A LONG WAY BACK

Anna
Best Wishes

Mike Welch

A LONG WAY BACK

A Novel

Mike Holst

iUniverse, Inc.
New York Lincoln · Shanghai

A LONG WAY BACK

iUniverse books may be ordered through booksellers or by contacting:

iUniverse
2021 Pine Lake Road, Suite 100
Lincoln, NE 68512
www.iuniverse.com
1-800-Authors (1-800-288-4677)

Because of the dynamic nature of the Internet, any Web addresses or links contained in this book may have changed since publication and may no longer be valid.

This is a work of fiction. All of the characters, names, incidents, organizations, and dialogue in this novel are either the products of the author's imagination or are used fictitiously.

ISBN: 978-0-595-44945-3 (pbk)
ISBN: 978-0-595-89267-9 (ebk)

Printed in the United States of America

This book is dedicated to Kitty. Without her hard work and encouragement it would not have been possible. She truly is my love, my life, my everything.

FOREWORD

The vast wilderness area of northeastern Minnesota remains today as it was hundreds of years ago. Rocky cliffs surround bodies of sparkling clean water, and cascading streams so pure you can drink from them, wind their way from lake to lake, teeming with fish and wildlife. Gigantic first growth forests cover the area providing shelter and safe haven for birds and animals that have maintained a delicate balance with nature for centuries. The air is clean and the environment is quiet. Only the sounds that belong there exist.

Every effort has been made to keep this pristine wilderness from succumbing to the pressure of a society that clamors to infiltrate the area with motorized recreational vehicles, lodges and cabins. There are lumber companies that have long wanted to strip the land of timber and leave it crisscrossed with roads and trails. Development has been effectively stopped in its tracks around the perimeter. Through careful management as a national park area, the public has been allowed in, but only with the same primitive means that our ancestors were forced to use hundreds of years ago. For that reason most of the area remains free of man and the pollution that is inherent to civilization.

Despite all of its beauty, it can be a wild and mysterious place to traverse and live in. The rules of survival are the same ones Mother Nature has handed down through the ages. Those who find themselves alone in this great area can find themselves in the fight of their lives. They will effectively be reduced to the level of the animals of the forests, without the natural survival instincts these animals possess, and that is a great handicap. This story is about such an ordeal with a few roadblocks thrown in. It is also about some unexpected help from one of Mother Natures finest. It is a work of fiction, but it very well could happen.

PROLOGUE

▼

The flash from the bolt of lightning had been seen only a split second ahead of the jolt that shook the small aircraft from the prop to the tail. It was almost as if the great god Thor, the god of thunder himself, had been hiding behind that swirling green bank of clouds off to the right and had reached down, pointed his fickle finger of authority, and tried to knock them from the sky. One thing was certain; it had stopped them dead in their tracks.

At first, the plane seemed to respond to his frantic controlling, but then it was deathly quiet and Arnie realized he no longer had an engine … that it was just the wind whistling by them as they glided slowly to earth that was turning the prop around.

With a quick look at the map and the compass on the dash, the realization grew within him that all of the fancy avionics were useless to him. The gauges had all failed. Nothing worked. An acidic smoke smell filled the cockpit, burning their eyes, making it hard to see.

The blue and white Cessna was now essentially a glider, and they were on a straight trip into whatever waited below them in the darkness. There would be no once around to look the landing site over … this was it.

Quick flashes from his past were blinking through Arnie's mind in those few moments on the way down. The memories of flying with his dad in the yellow Piper Cub when he was just a small boy, his nose pressed against the cold window glass feeling the vibrations of the engine through his forehead, and looking for landmarks below. Marveling how they could compete with the bird's way up here, and examining the bottoms of the clouds up close. He remembered his father's face, always determined, always serious, but always at ease up there in the sky.

Arnie remembered those long talks at the kitchen table with Mom in her colorful aprons. The smell of homemade bread coming from the hot oven, and the table covered with fresh cinnamon rolls.

There were his high school sports days … the long hours spent on the rink playing hockey, his cheeks rosy red with cold and exertion. He was a fiery competitor and victory was always his ultimate goal.

Then his graduation from high school and his parents overwhelming pride when he got a scholarship to the University of Minnesota for journalism. Graduation came once more, and with it a good job offer that he turned down to be a freelance writer. He was his own person and wanted no outside controls.

There was his disappointing marriage to Ann, and his son Timmy's birth. Ann deserted him and the child, and then came the inevitable subsequent trials and joys that are inherent with raising a handicapped child. There was a brief thought of the home he had built with his own hands on Sunrise Lake, the culmination of a lifetime dream. His writing career and his job, with all of that freedom of self-expression Arnie felt so strong about.

Then there was his life turning around with the addition of Julie. Julie had brought a whole new perspective to his life. She had made life fun again and had brought technicolor into the black and white existence he had been mired in. She made him laugh again, but most of all she made him love again, when he had forgotten how. He drew life from her and she from him, but right this moment as Arnie looked over at her in the smoky near darkness of the cockpit, her mouth and eyes were wide open in fear.

"We're all going to die Arnie." The words were literally screamed at him, but he had barely heard Julie, because he was busy searching in the darkness for a safe place to touch down. He had been a survivor all of his life and he was not going to quit now.

CHAPTER 1

▼

Julie awakened startled and shaken. More afraid than she could ever recall, and had she actually screamed? It had seemed so real that she must have, and it was still echoing in the back of her head. Trembling, Julie looked down at Arnie sleeping with his back towards her, seemingly undisturbed. The red numerals on the clock on the nightstand said 2:45 a.m.

She was sitting up in bed with the pillow pressed to her chest by her knees, and her shaking hands were balled into tight fists clutching the sheet underneath her. Her nightshirt was wet with sweat and her short red hair seemed plastered to the back of her head.

Slipping carefully out of bed Julie crept downstairs in the early morning darkness, and walked over to the large front window. The only light in the room was coming from a near full moon shining down from a cloudless sky. That bright celestial light was centered in the window glass and left a mystical lighted path from the house, across the still cold waters of the lake, then disappeared into the dark forests on the other side.

The yellow plane still bobbed in the water next to the dock making its own little waves. Had it been it a premonition or were the fears that she carried around for so long just playing games with her? She hated Arnie's old vintage plane and lived in fear of what could happen, but didn't know what to do about it.

Julie retreated to the back of the room and peeked in on Timmy. She heard his shallow breathing and she could hear Jake moving around in the porch his claws clicking on the hardwood floors.

Returning upstairs she changed her nightclothes and crawled back into bed, spooning with Arnie. He pushed his bottom into her and grunted. It was all the comfort and reassurance she was going to get from him.

Julie heard the steady drone of the airplane engine off to the west somewhere. It reminded her of an angry mosquito buzzing around on a dark summer night, searching for an uncovered shoulder or a bare neck to feast on. She walked over to the window and parted the curtains, trying to see over the treetops for some sign of him, but when he came from that direction the trees hid him. It has been said, "Some people can not see the trees for the forest." For Julie, she couldn't see anything for the 'forest' they lived in. *It has to be Arnie,* she thought.

The bright yellow plane seemed to burst out of nowhere, several feet above the trees tops, and settling onto the calm waters just beyond the end of the dock with a whoosh and a splash. Two fat greenhead ducks that had been swimming there beat a noisy quacking retreat to the center of the lake. It was Arnie's usual way of arriving back home with some of his carefree theatrics and acrobatics thrown in. As he spun the plane around to taxi to shore, Julie could see that big foolish grin of his through the tiny dirty windshield. "*Goof ball*" she thought and laughed.

"Timmy, daddy's home. Let's go meet him. This way, come, hurry." Timmy who had been sitting amid a pile of toys was also smiling broadly but said nothing, and probably wouldn't. That didn't mean he wasn't happy … he was just locked up in his own little world where he had been from birth. Jumping up from his toys he ran and grabbed Julie's hand.

Hand in hand, the young boy and the petite redhead with her pixie haircut ran down the carefully laid limestone blocks to the dock, arriving just as the engine sputtered to a stop and the prop feathered. For a second it was quiet, and an elusive wisp of dying exhaust found its way out of the pipe from the engine. Then the waves from the plane's floats broke nosily on shore and Arnie kicked the squeaky door open. His high laced up lumberjack boot was the first thing to emerge, and then he stepped out on the float squinting in the bright sunlight.

"Damn, what a day to fly. You know what Julie; it's the only way to really enjoy this land and how it really looks. When you're on the ground you see only a small part of the puzzle, but up there the whole world is laid out in front of you like a big old picture book."

He stepped from the float to the dock and she encircled him with her arms, putting her hands in his back pockets. She kissed him quickly twice, wrinkling her nose. His mustache tickled her nose. "Did you get any writing done, or were you too busy playing the Red Barron?"

"Yes I did, weeks worth my little love, but mostly I just sat around trying to picture you and Timmy there, wishing you were with me."

Julie laughed and let go of him. Timmy crawled in between them and hugged Arnie's legs. "That's what I love about you, Arnie Bottelmiller. You are so full of it. Come on up to the house. Suppers ready."

Arnie picked Timmy up and then blowing bubbles in his tummy as they walked up to the house, he put him up on his shoulders. Timmy squealed and laughed his hands gripping Arnie's curly hair.

If there was anything Arnie Bottelmiller loved more than flying, it was not very evident to those who knew him best. Well, maybe it was Julie and Timmy, on a good day. She was the love of his life, as was his son, but Julie had long ago conceded that she was playing second fiddle to an airplane and always would be. It wasn't only the flying, but also his love for the vast wilderness of northern Minnesota that Arnie couldn't get enough of.

He had moved to the fringes of this wilderness eleven years ago and built his home out of white pine logs that had grown on his land. His wasn't the only home on tiny Sunrise Lake, but you could count the rest of them on one hand, and in the winter his was the only one inhabited.

Arnie looked every bit the outdoorsman he was. He stood six foot tall with broad shoulders and a barrel chest tapering down to a thirty-four-inch waist. His hands were not the hands of the writer he was, but the hands of a man who cut wood to heat his house and spent many hours fishing in the blistering sun. Arnie's complexion was ruddy from the winter winds, and permanently tanned from the summer sun. His face sported a short trim beard that was just now starting to show a few flecks of gray, and he wore his reddish hair long. His natural curls, along with the youthful grin that was almost always on his face, still gave him a hint of boyishness.

Arnie made a good living writing an outdoor column that was published in most of the papers in northern Minnesota. He was also a well-known activist, working to preserve the boundary water wilderness of the region. His column was published twice weekly and he had his own following who bought the paper only to read Arnie's column. For many of them the rest of the paper was used to wrap their fish guts in.

Although his writings occasionally carried political overtones, he tried to stay out of that field. Mostly they provided his readers with information on the day-to-day events that went on in the boundary water area. If you read between the lines you could always feel his love for the country and its inhabitants. Arnie was also the resident expert on the lives and ways of the birds, fish and animals that lived in this vast wilderness. Never tiring of taking their pictures, he observed the wildlife for endless hours in their natural habitat. He often wrote his column as he leaned against a tree on a rocky cliff overlooking one of the thousands of lakes encompassing the area, while his old yellow plane bobbed on the waves below him.

"I write best when I am being part of what I write about," he had said many times.

Because Arnie knew the area better than the rangers and conservation people who cared for it, he was often called on to render his opinion about how to best tackle the difficult environmental issues.

His love for the area coupled with his love of flying beckoned him into this wilderness, and several times a week he would land his little Piper float plane on one of the lakes that he chose to study. He would often tie his plane up at a small island and stay the night gathering information or just enjoying the peace of mind that blessed him out there.

Julie Feldman was Arnie's constant companion, except when he flew. She was a nervous flyer and didn't feel comfortable in small planes. Oh, she went with him when she had to, but if there was a way out of it she usually found it.

Arnie met Julie seven years ago, not long after his divorce from his first wife Ann, who had deserted him and their year-old-son. Ann, wasn't necessarily a bad person, she just never got over the fact that their son was born mentally handicapped. She had been so proud to give Arnie a son, but their little boy's flaw was her downfall.

Working at home, Arnie was able to care for Timmy and still make a living doing the work he loved. For a couple of years Timmy prevented him from traveling, but then as he grew older Arnie could be seen strapping the young boy in the co-pilot seat of his plane and flying away to some far away lake.

At first Julie and Arnie's relationship had been somewhat rocky, but like so many love affairs that eventually blossomed, it took only persistence and a brief adjustment period. Julie did not immediately share Arnie's love of the great outdoors, but as time passed she came to love the area as much as he did. It was just the flying that she could not buy into.

She was born and raised in Blue Lake, but as a young girl just out of school her first desire had been to leave, that is, until she met Arnie and his son.

Julie became very fond of Timmy, often babysitting him when Arnie was taking care of business. She had been raised with a handicapped younger brother who died when she was just a teenager. She never got over her loss, and Timmy filled that void in her life. She saw Timmy as a challenge she had to take on for her brother's sake.

About a year into their relationship Julie left her cozy apartment in Blue Lake and moved in with Arnie. Although they talked about marriage they never did take that final step. Getting married hadn't been a contentious issue, but they did talk about it from time to time.

Arnie loved Julie for who she was, but he also loved her for the way she took to Timmy and loved and cared for him as if he were her own. He rewrote his will, leaving everything he owned to Julie in the event of his death, as long as she cared for Timmy until he was an adult. In her mind, Julie felt they were already married. She even had Arnie buy her a plain gold band that she wore everywhere she went. If he ever asked her to marry him, there was no doubt that she would say yes, but it was up to him and she was not going to influence that decision, one way or the other.

Arnie loved Julie for who she was, but he also loved her for the way she took to Timmy and loved and cared for him as if he were her own.

Julie was attractive and athletic, and took good care of herself. Her trim figure was rock hard. She worked out every day in the three-season-porch attached to the house. It was filled with stair steppers, stationary bikes, and other pieces of workout equipment. She wore her red hair short and seldom wore makeup. She didn't need it; her skin was flawless. She loved to swim, and despite the coldness of the lake, she swam daily in the summer.

The log home they lived in was not big by most people's standards, but Arnie had added onto it twice since he built it. He remodeled a downstairs room into a bedroom for Timmy and shortly after Julie moved in, he added the three-season porch. The front of the house had huge windows overlooking the lake from the large family room. From high on the rocky bluff one could see across the entire lake. In the morning the rising sun would shine brightly right into the front of the house, bathing the sturdy log home in its warm rays. Arnie never needed an alarm clock. He got up when the sun welcomed him to another day. Timmy's bedroom, the family room, kitchen and bath were located downstairs. Upstairs in the loft were Arnie and Julie's bedroom and Arnie's office. Here he built a dormer so as he wrote, he could see out on the area he loved so much.

Timmy's other love and protector was Jake. Two years ago Arnie had brought home a Golden Labrador puppy for Timmy's Christmas gift and now they were inseparable. One big dissimilarity between the two was the fact that, as much as

Timmy feared the water, Jake loved it. As a retriever, he had been bred for the water and it was in his bloodline. Because of his disgusting habit of hunting and bringing home small dead animals and fish on his adventures, Jake was often limited to the three-season porch, so he and Timmy spent a lot of time in there together.

Jake also loved to fly and ride in the car, so wherever Arnie and Timmy went, Jake went too as Timmy would not leave home without him. Arnie had made a harness system for Jake to wear in the plane, but in the car he bounded from one seat to the next, keeping a close eye out for whatever moved. Jake was also a comfort to Julie when Arnie was gone. He was a very alert watchdog and would bark whenever anything outside disturbed him. Through his adventures he learned to leave porcupines and skunks alone. A face full of quills from a porcupine's tail and a near miss by a mama skunk's spray had taught him that lesson, but he still delighted in chasing squirrels, rabbits, and an occasional deer or bear. He never chased them far, just far enough to let them know they weren't welcome around there.

CHAPTER 2

▼

It was Tuesday morning, and Arnie slipped out of bed just as the sun peeked over the horizon to make his way down to the kitchen to put on the coffeepot. He had to be out of there by six a.m. to make an eight a.m. meeting in Duluth with his favorite editor, and then he was going out to Sky High Airfield in the nearby town of Superior, Wisconsin, to look at a new airplane. Shirley Capes, the editor of the paper had told him about the plane a few weeks back, and Arnie had her arrange a meeting with the owner to look it over, although he seriously doubted he could afford it.

With the coffee brewing, Arnie peeked in on Timmy, who was sleeping soundly on his back, his hand clutching an old Barney doll that would normally have been something for someone much younger but was Timmy's constant sleeping companion. He watched him for a few minutes trying to imagine how different it could have been with Timmy if—but then left feeling selfish for thinking that way. He went to put out fresh water and food for Jake who had been curled up on the old couch in the porch. Jake's tail wagging against the wall threatened to wake up everybody and knock the lamp off the end table, so Arnie stopped to settle him down before he left.

Coffee in hand, he went back upstairs and took clean underwear and socks out of the dresser before heading back down to the bathroom. Julie was sleeping on her back with one bare shoulder and part of her breast showing in the early morning light. Arnie pulled the covers up tightly around her neck and kissed her forehead before he left. Julie stirred but didn't wake up.

The hot water felt so good, but he was running late so he showered quickly, brushed his teeth and got dressed. He went back up for his outer clothes and then into his office to grab his briefcase. He stopped and kissed Julie on the forehead again, which brought a sleepy smile this time and a, "Please be careful, I love you."

"Love you too sweetheart," Arnie said. "Have a good day." He stopped to look in on Timmy once more. He hadn't moved and the look on his face was angelic, not Timmy's usual demeanor when he was awake. Patting Jake on the head, Arnie was out the door and down the stone path to the lake.

The sun was just coming up, and there was a low fog over the lake, brought on by the cold September air meeting the warmer water. A loon gave an eerie cry somewhere out on the water, and a muskrat swam by the end of the dock before diving out of sight. The ripples from his dive in the calm water spread out in an ever-increasing pattern before they were absorbed and disappeared as quickly as they had come.

Arnie stood and drank it all in for a second, and then, putting his briefcase and coffee down on the dock, grabbed the rope and pulled the plane over to him. He used an old towel to wipe the dew off the windows and then checked the engine oil. He had just worked on the plane yesterday, so he was pretty confident everything was good to go.

Standing on the float, he opened the door and put his stuff inside before climbing aboard. The engine started with a roar, and Arnie gave it a minute to warm up before casting off the rope and slowly taxing down the shoreline and out onto the lake. The water was perfectly calm, and the planes floats made tiny ripples that formed into miniature waves that headed for shore. He would be gone before they ever got there.

As he turned the nose of the plane out into the middle of the lake, he looked over his shoulder one last time and could see Julie standing in the window clutching her robe to her chest and waving at him. Arnie waved back and opened the throttle. He taxied across the surface until he reached airspeed, pulled back on the wheel, and the Piper was airborne, maybe for the last time with Arnie at the throttle. He slowly circled the lake to gain some altitude, and then set his course for Duluth, a hundred miles to the east.

There wasn't a cloud to be seen in the sky above, or on the horizon, so Arnie settled back with his coffee cup and enjoyed the day. He felt so free up here four thousand feet above the land he loved so much. Beneath him, the lakes of the boundary waters showed up as if they had been painted in a special aqua blue color, to contrast with the evergreens. The fall colors were starting to show up: bright red on the maples and oaks, and yellow on the birch and aspen. Far off to his right, below him, he could make out the distinct V pattern of a flight of Canadian geese, and he made a mental note to keep a close watch for any more, as they could be deadly to an aircraft.

The flat forested area gave way to rocky cliffs, and on the horizon Arnie started to make out the vast expanse of Lake Superior. He flew over Duluth, and then established radio contact with the airport, telling them he would be landing at his usual place, which was set aside for float planes to land on the lake. He then cut his airspeed, set his flaps and brought the little Piper in with a feather touch landing that hardly rippled a hair on his head. He taxied to the pier where a helper assisted him in tying up the plane. Shirley was waiting for him by her car as Arnie cut the engine and stepped off the float, walking briskly down the pier to meet her. It was colder here than at home because of the breeze off the big lake, and he stopped to put on his jacket which he had flung over his shoulder.

"Hi, stranger," Shirley said as they got in her big white Lincoln.

"Morning, Shirley," Arnie answered. "Business before pleasure I presume, right?"

"Right you are, my friend. Let's go, we're late." She left heading toward town and onto the road heading away from the airport.

Arnie had known Shirley for many years, and although she normally didn't pick him up at the dock, they had been on plenty of automobile rides together. Shirley had been a beautiful woman at one time, and even now, if you got beyond the wrinkles and gray hair, you could still see some of that beauty. She still had a good figure and enough of those $800 business suits to go around for a month without wearing the same one twice. If there was anything bad about her it was the cigarette that seemed to be permanent fixture, either in her mouth or in her hand. Even now she drove with one eye closed because of the smoke drifting in her face from the Camel in the corner of her mouth. Her voice was husky from her smoking and she coughed into her sleeve before quickly saying. "Excuse me, these damn allergies."

They crossed the bridge into downtown Duluth making small talk about the weather and the coming winter. Pulling up to the newspaper office, she parked the Lincoln in front of a large white sign that read, **Reserved for Shirley Capes, Managing Editor**.

Arnie stepped ahead of her and opened the door. She was the boss, but she still liked to be treated like a lady. Shirley smiled and said" Thanks," before starting started up the stairs ahead of him to the office area, talking over her shoulder as she went. "Someday Arnie I'm going to convince you to work exclusively for me." She turned as she reached the landing expecting an answer, but he only smiled standing down a step behind her.

"You were looking at my butt instead of listening weren't you?" She quipped.

Arnie laughed, but said nothing

The meeting had been set up with all the columnists and was held two or three times a year to go over goals and changes in the way they operated. Arnie sold his column to several papers, but this was the big one, so he was always included in the meetings even though he wasn't directly an employee.

Arnie enjoyed his freedom and independence too much to be an employee, and he was afraid of the censorship it might present to him. Most of the meeting was reserved for the full-time writers from the paper, and Arnie sat at the table as an interested spectator. For the most part Shirley ran the meeting with limited input from the editorial staff and those she depended on to run the newspaper.

The meeting was concluded by noon, and Shirley dismissed everyone, but held her hand up when Arnie started to rise as if to say, wait a second. He sat back down. When everyone else had left, she lit up the cigarette she had held in her hand for an hour and inhaled deeply.

"Arnie," she began, "I want to discuss a business proposition with you. You know that I want you to work exclusively for my paper. That's no secret and never has been. You and I have talked about this many times in the past and have never come to an agreement. I'm a writer too, Arnie. I understand what you are afraid of losing, but I think you do can do so much better if you will just let me help you. There's a big market for what you write and I know how to tap into it. Enough said about that." She could sense his reluctance and didn't want to provoke it.

She sat on the corner of the table in front of him one leg dangling over the end of it.

"In a few minutes I am going to take you out to see that airplane I told you about, and I think you are going to like it a lot." She stopped talking momentarily to crush out her cigarette and light another one. "I know how you like to fly, my friend, and this is the Cadillac of airplanes. This thing damn near flies itself, Arnie, but it's not cheap, and I think you know what its worth."

Shirley reached down and tilted his chin up so he was looking right at her.

"Here's my proposition, Arnie Bottelmiller, so listen up. Number one, I am prepared to increase the amount we pay you by twenty-five percent." She hesitated for a second as a staff person walked by. "Oh hell, I'm going to do that anyway, but listen close to the rest of this."

She had got down off the table and walked to the other side of it, and was now standing with her arms crossed over her chest.

"Number two," she resumed, "I will continue to let your column be published in any newspaper it is now published in." She paused for a second and then continued. "But they buy it from me, not you. I will increase your exposure in other papers one hundred percent and you can take that to the bank."

Arnie was shaking his head from side to side indicating he was opposed to that, but he said nothing and continued to make eye contact.

"Don't get too excited now, because this is the kicker, Arnie Bottelmiller and it's a big one." She was leaning over the table her face inches from his. Her tobacco-tainted breath was mixed with a sweet flowery perfume he had not noticed until now.

"I am making this offer, Arnie, before you ever see this plane. I don't want your decision colored by your first impression of it. If you don't want a part of this deal, you tell me before we leave this building."

"I'm listening," he said.

"I will buy it for you free and clear." Shirley straightened back up and crossed her arms again. Her face wore a look of grim seriousness.

Arnie swallowed and shifted nervously in his chair. He was rarely intimidated by anyone, but she had him by the short hairs now, and he needed to be careful.

"You flying that forty-year-old Piper Cub around scares the shit out of me." Shirley had sat down across the table from him with her hand on his arm. "I know I'm not going to get you to quit flying, so the least I can do is get your stubborn ass into something safe."

Arnie listened intently, and with a nervous smile playing at the corners of his mouth, he looked at Shirley and said. "For the first time, I am not going to say no immediately. I think if I did consider this, we'd need to talk some more about some censorship issues that I know will surface down the road. You and I are on the opposite side of the issue more time than not."

Changing the flow of the conversation he said, "Give me one of those Camels." Arnie rarely smoked, and never in front of Julie, but he did chew Beechnut chewing tobacco when he was outside, and she put up with that. Right now he needed a little nicotine to clear his head.

They shared a match and both lit up. Then Shirley continued. "Arnie, I 'm not going to tell you what to write. I haven't in the past and I am not going to now, and if you need that in writing I will do it."

Arnie thought for a moment and then said, "Let's go look at that plane, after you buy me lunch Boss."

As they left the office Shirley grabbed his arm in hers and quipped. "You walk beside me, not behind me, you pervert."

Arnie howled with laughter.

They drove down to Grandma's restaurant on the waterfront, scattering a flock of seagulls in the parking lot. Grandma's was an icon; it was as much Duluth as the hills and ore docks that bordered the city from one side to the other. Inside the sprawling restaurant the walls were covered with sports memorabilia and pictures of the many people who had won Grandma's marathon. The race they sponsored was run every spring along the beautiful North Shore Drive that wound north of Duluth some two hundred miles to the Canadian border.

They didn't talk any more about the proposal while they ate, but instead discussed the subjects that were near and dear to all northern Minnesotans—the lakes, the forests and wildlife, the dwindling industry and the newspaper.

Shirley had taken over the paper when her husband Edgar died in a plane crash in the late eighties. Maybe that was why she was worried about Arnie's welfare. Aside from that, she enjoyed Arnie's company as well as his writing. She was past the age of crushes, but if she ever found another man he would be more like Arnie, not Edgar, who had tended to be stuffy.

Finished with lunch, they went back out to Shirley's car and drove out to the airport. The newspaper owned a hangar there and it seemed odd that the plane they didn't own was parked inside and their corporate jet was sitting out.

When Arnie walked through the door into the hangar, he was behind a wall for the first few feet, but as he rounded the corner, there it was, right in front of him. The metal arc lights inside the hangar bathed the shiny aircraft in a heavenly radiant glow as if it had a spotlight shining directly on it. The floor, which was painted white, added to the ambience, and for a moment Arnie just stood and drank it all in, Shirley standing right behind him.

The plane was a beautiful almost new Cessna Skyhawk, white with dark blue trim. Arnie walked over and opened the front door cautiously. The black leather seats looked and felt rich, and the carpeting was soft and plush. Even used, it still had that new smell to it. The dash was loaded with instruments and a lot of modern avionics Arnie had never seen or used before.

"Go ahead and get in," Shirley said.

Arnie did, and he was like a kid on a fire truck as he ran his hands over everything. It had four seats and room for cargo behind them. It was the nicest small plane he had ever sat in. "How much are they asking?" he asked Shirley through the open door below him.

"You don't want to know," she answered, "but I told you I would buy it for you, so why ask?"

Arnie jumped back down to the ground and walked around the outside, slowly letting his hand feel every part of the plane. He ended up next to Shirley, speechless for the moment as he stood and looked it over some more. "When do you want to know?" he finally asked.

"Now," Shirley said.

His better judgment said no, but his heart said yes, and after a brief tussle, his heart won out. "Only if you put floats on it for me." He reached in his pocket for his Beechnut tobacco and filled his cheek.

CHAPTER 3

▼

It was four-thirty before they got all the papers signed, and Shirley brought Arnie back to his old yellow plane. The wind had come up and the big lake was getting wild. He was parked behind a breakwater in a protective cove, but the weather still made him nervous. He was anxious to get going.

Arnie sat in the plane while it warmed up and thought about what he had just done. The Cessna was beautiful and everything he had ever dreamed of, but so was his writing freedom. He hoped he wasn't going to regret what had happened. He dialed his cell phone to tell Julie he was on his way, but she didn't answer the phone. He left her a message saying he should be home in an hour or so.

Watching Shirley walk back to her car after she had left him, he'd thought for a moment he could detect a bit of a victory smirk. The wind was blowing hard, her long hair was whipping around her head, and her coattails lifted just enough for Arnie to see she still had a nice body for a woman her age. *She must have been a good bang in her day*, Arnie thought, and then laughing to himself just as quickly, shook his head to clear the thought. *I am a pervert*, he thought, and laughed again.

Still smiling, he taxied around for take off and cleared it with the local authorities. The new plane would be delivered to him next week after they had it outfitted with floats. He would be given a few lessons on flying it as part of the deal. Arnie was qualified for instrument flying, and had on one occasion flown a similar plane that belonged to a friend in his hometown.

Julie had gone down to the lake to fish with Timmy and was on the end of the dock with a fish on her line when her phone rang. She wanted this fish for supper, so she let the call go to the message center while she pulled in a nice four-pound walleye. Timmy jumped and clapped with glee, hugging Julie when he saw the fish, almost knocking both of them and the fish in the lake. Jake didn't know what the excitement was about, but he got in the spirit and ran up and down the dock barking and finished with a jump off the end to show his approval. After paddling slowly to shore, Jake shook off, and a spray of cold lake water soaked both Julie and Timmy, prompting Julie to scream, "Jake, you asshole, get out of here!" He sulked up to the house, not sure what had brought on that outburst, but knowing he had gotten hell for something.

Julie took Timmy by the hand and they headed for the house to dry off. Julie saw Timmy as a special child, not a handicapped child. He brought a new kind of joy into her life that she had once known with her brother, but had forgotten existed. She hoisted him on her shoulders and strode with an exaggerated stomp as they walked to the house. "You are getting so big, my little friend, that I'm not sure old Julie's back is going to take much more of this."

Timmy giggled as only a kid can as she dumped him into a hammock that was just outside the front door and then crawled in with him tickling him to keep him going. They would catch a little sun and watch for Arnie. Then, remembering the phone call, she started to get back up. *She had better check the recorder. No it could wait.* She buried her face in Timmy's hair and held him close.

The flight back was uneventful, and with a forty-mile-an-hour tailwind, Arnie was home in record time, but not before he had spent time thinking about the things that were so important in his life. As nice as this new plane was, his family and his writing was all he really lived for. New planes were a dime a dozen, but women like Julie and sons like Timmy were hard to find.

He circled the lake to lose some altitude, and then banking to the left, brought the little Piper Cub down and passed the end of the dock where Julie was just finishing cleaning her fish. She stopped long enough to throw Arnie a rope as he came up next to the dock and stepped out on the float.

"Hey, what's that shit-eating grin for, Arnie Bottelmiller?" She laughed as he stepped up on the dock.

Arnie smiled and picked up her fish. Putting his other arm around her he said, "Tell you at supper, babe."

Arnie explained everything to Julie, and she was happy that he was getting a safer plane, which they would never have been able to afford, but on the other hand she was still suspicious of the deal. "I don't know, Arnie. I just don't know.

You've always prided yourself on the fact that you were an independent writer, not part of a syndicate. I hope you don't live to regret this."

Arnie could see genuine concern on her face, and he knew he was going to have to work hard to show her that her fears were not justifiable. Or were they? Now he was getting confused.

Arnie did not continue the discussion with Julie and after supper he went into his home office to prepare the next day's column. He was disappointed that she hadn't been more supportive, but on the other hand he valued and respected her opinion.

He always had to drive into town so the column could be faxed from the bank where Julie worked to the papers where it was published. Sometimes Julie took it to work with her and did it for him. It was a good thing he had written most of it yesterday, as he was having trouble concentrating tonight. By ten p.m. he finished and went downstairs for a beer and a snack.

Julie was curled up on the sofa sleeping, a book in her hand and Jake's head in her lap. The fire in the woodstove was nearly out, and Arnie brought in more wood from outside and stocked it for the night. On his second trip out, he heard the mournful howl of a wolf across the lake as if it were saying, "I'm over here," and he noted the mirror-image reflection of the trees in the still waters. It was chilly and before long the crushing winds of winter would hide the lake under its winter shell of ice for another five months. Arnie's flying would have to be out of the airport in town.

Back inside he picked Timmy up off the floor and carried him into his room. Timmy was small for his age, but he was still getting to be an armful for Arnie to carry to bed. Arnie pulled off Timmy's jeans and socks. He put his pajama bottoms on, skipping the top and letting him sleep in his T-shirt. He sat down on the bed beside him for a moment and ran his hands through Timmy's hair, wishing as he had a thousand times that he had been born without any problems, but then realized again how blessed he was to have him at all. He kissed his son good night, turned on the night-light, and left the room.

Julie was awake when he returned to the porch. Arnie sat down next to her and started nibbling on her ear, but she playfully pushed him away. "You got one screwing today, Arnie, and that's enough." She laughed.

For a second, Arnie's mood grew somber. Not getting laid was one thing, but Julie thinking he had gotten the shaft from Shirley was something else. "You wait till you see this plane, sweetheart, and you'll change your mind," he said at last.

Julie took Timmy to Arnie's mother's house the next morning on her way to work. Arnie was going to write in the morning, and then he was going to fly over to another lake to look at some erosion problems he was writing about. The lake was not in the boundary water area but it was uninhabited and as usual, developers were pushing a road into the area with no regard for the land. The road had washed out into the lake in several spots and left huge scars in the hillsides. Arnie was not against the development, but the way it was being done. *Oh bullshit, he thought. Who am I fooling? I don't want them here, period,* but he was powerless to stop them.

Arnie took pictures of the damage and walked briefly through the area. He had hunted here when he was a kid and remembered when it was pristine wilderness. Soon it would be full of speedboats and wave runners humming around like a bunch of angry mosquitoes. Arnie and his two neighbors owned most of the land on their lake and were united in the fight to not let it happen there.

The following Monday morning, Shirley called and said that Dan Post, a pilot for the newspaper, was coming in for a couple of days to deliver the plane and get Arnie up to speed on it. Arnie was outside playing with Timmy when he first heard the drone, and then saw the Cessna come over the treetops and circle the lake. He and Timmy went and stood on the dock, waving their arms to let the pilot know which of the three houses was theirs.

Dan Post was a man out of his environment and seemed in awe when he saw the lake and Arnie's place. Dan was not an outdoorsman; in fact, he had been born and raised in Minneapolis. He served in the Air Force for twenty years, and then moved to Duluth to go to work for the paper and a charter company as a pilot. He wasn't married and never had been, but not for a lack of good looks. He had curly black hair and a dark complexion that hinted at a Greek or Italian heritage. He was also remarkably trim, and his clothes looked like they had been tailored to fit him.

Arnie had forgotten for a second what the Cessna looked like, but it all came back now and sitting by his dock it sure looked good. Last night he pulled the Piper down the shoreline a ways, and it looked a little sad sitting there. So far he hadn't made any plans as to what he would do with it.

Dan stepped off the plane, stood on the dock and introduced himself. He stared, fascinated at the surrounding countryside while they got acquainted, and then Arnie brought him up to the house. Dan said he was familiar with Arnie's column and his other writings and told him what a big fan he was.

Arnie nodded his appreciation and put his arm around Timmy. "I'm anxious to get in the air, Dan," Arnie said. "Let's run into town, and I'll get my mother to watch Timmy while we go up. Julie's working right now, but I'll let her know so she can bring him home with her tonight."

Arnie explained about Timmy's handicap, and Dan was sympathetic. He had a brother who had been injured as a child in an accident. Although not as handicapped as Timmy, he still lived at home with Dan's parents.

Arnie's other vehicle, when he needed one, was a twenty-year-old Ford pickup that was held together with duct tape and wire. "I apologize for the dirty truck," he said, explaining that with the plane he didn't need it much because Julie's Jeep was usually available.

There was not much chance for conversation on the way to town, as the old pickup needed a muffler and made a lot of noise. Timmy loved to ride in the truck though, and laughed and pounded on the dash between Arnie and Dan. Both men were amused at Timmy's glee and laughed with him.

It was only twelve miles to Arnie's mom's house on the outskirts of town, so that was their first stop. It was a quaint little house tucked back on a long lot full of evergreen trees. A big garden was off to the right as you came up the driveway, and right now it held the remnants of last years harvest, mostly rotted squash and tomatoes on dead dried up vines.

Timmy loved his grandmother and considered her his other mother. She was nearly as wide as she was tall and wore her hair in a rolled-up bun on the back of her head. The house was full of good cooking smells, and Arnie nosed around the kitchen for a second before he left, stealing a handful of cookies for him and Dan, who had elected to stay in the truck, "Thanks, Mom," Arnie said. "This came up kind of fast."

"Arnold, you know I never mind taking care of Timmy. You just behave yourself and be careful in that new plane."Arnie gave her a hug and left, the storm door banging behind him as he ran down the steps.

They stopped at the bank to see Julie, and Arnie had a fax to send. While Arnie played with her fax machine, Julie gave Dan a big smile and told him how excited Arnie was about his new plane.

Dan seemed shy at first but Julie made him feel at ease in just a few minutes. She could be coy around other men. It was one of her good points, but it made Arnie a little jealous from time to time.

Arnie asked Julie to pick up some things at the market on her way home and told her where Timmy was. "Mom says he can stay if you'd like, but I'll leave that up to you." When they left, two of the girls in the bank rushed to Julie's desk to find out who the hunk was, but she just laughed.

They were quickly back home and Arnie helped Dan fuel up the plane while Dan went over the safety checks with him. Arnie was like a kid on Christmas morning with a new toy, and he inspected every nook and cranny of the new plane.

It was a great fall day. The sun was warm and the surface of the lake was smooth, broken up only by a few leaves floating on the top of the water. They sat in the cockpit for some time as Dan explained the new instruments that Arnie had trained on before, but did not have in his old plane. The engine was very quiet compared to the Piper, and the cabin was comfortable and roomy, and the radio was much clearer and had more range. Avionics had come a long way in the last twenty years.

"I'm just here to watch you, it's your baby," Dan said. "Let's go up."

Arnie smiled and taxied the plane around. He opened the throttle, and they were hurtling across the lake and into the air so fast it was surprising. This plane was so responsive compared to the old one.

They flew north over the wilderness area and made a few practice landings on lakes that Arnie was familiar with. He practiced flying with the instruments only, wearing a special mask Dan made him wear that let him see only the instrument panel. They flew as high as they dared, and as low as was legal, and then as dusk was coming on, they headed for home.

Dan, Arnie, and Julie had a great evening. Julie cooked a roast and baked fresh bread. They sat in the porch until late, swapping stories, telling jokes, and drinking some of Arnie's home-brewed beer. They didn't get a lot of company, so it was a treat for Arnie and Julie to entertain.

The next morning, all three of them flew to Duluth to bring Dan back. For Julie it was a treat to get away, even though flying still made her very nervous. She had to admit, though, that flying in this plane was more comfortable and she felt less frightened.

They landed at the airport this time instead of on the water. This plane was built for both land and water landings Arnie called in on the radio when they were forty miles out and got clearance to land on runway four, which was reserved for small planes. He brought them down so smoothly that Dan patted him on the back and said, "There's not a lot more I can teach you, Arnie. You're a good pilot."

"Thanks, Dan," Arnie said, and winked at Julie. She smiled and made a point of pulling her shirt away from her chest several times rapidly to simulate her beating heart.

Dan was in a hurry to leave so they said their good-byes, and he left Arnie and Julie standing in the terminal.

"Hey, kid, let's get a bite to eat and I'll take you shopping," Arnie whispered in her ear while he grabbed her butt. She squealed and slapped his hand.

They went to a café for lunch, and then Arnie called a cab and they went into town where they shopped for most of the afternoon. Tired and broke, they left the airport by the middle of the afternoon with the two backseats filled with packages. Julie didn't get to Duluth often, so she had enjoyed it while she could. Timmy was staying a couple nights at his grandmother's house, and it was nice to spend some time alone together.

Arnie needed to get home before dark. He had landed in the dark many times before, but until he was more used to the new plane, he didn't want to try it. The tower cleared them for takeoff, and Arnie was airborne, flying out over Lake Superior for a few miles to enjoy the scenery. Below them, a huge ore carrier lumbered across the lake heading toward the steel mills out east. Several smaller boats were giving it a wide berth as they headed into port. The Duluth skyline stretched in front of them as they pointed west and headed home.

The flight home was uneventful. The air was calm, the plane warm and quiet. They made plans to take a vacation the next week and fly to Thunder Bay Canada where Julie's folks had moved, and it was a chance to show off the new plane to them. They would take Timmy and Jake with them and make it a real family vacation. Arnie also had plans to take Julie to a special place where they had gone the night they met many years ago, and ask her to marry him. It was time. It was way overdue.

CHAPTER 4

▼

Arnie worked his butt off to get his columns ready for the next week's paper, and by Saturday afternoon he was done. It took a lot of work to verify every subject that he wrote about, but it was so important that the facts were there, and it was not just his opinion. Sometimes in the digging he would change his opinion as more facts came out, and many times he had given up or even scraped a project. It might mean a lot of work for nothing, but in the end it could save him from a lawsuit.

Sometimes Arnie was able to dig into his files if he got in a bind and recycle a bit from the past. Some subjects never died and deserved repeating. Writing was funny work. There were days when the words never stopped coming, and then there were days he felt lucky if he could remember his own name. In the end, it had to appeal to the readers or it was so much useless drivel and that drivel could ruin his reputation. Arnie knew a lot of people and had a lot of friends, so if he needed expert opinions on a subject he was always able to find what he needed.

Julie spent the morning packing clothes for all of them for the trip. She was excited about seeing her parents. It had been a while since they had been there. Because Jake's carrier took up so much room, she would have to pack carefully even though the new plane was bigger.

Arnie had taken the plane into town on Saturday and had it serviced, and when he came home, painted across the doors were the words *Miss Julie*. It brought a tear to her eye when she saw it. It was as if Arnie had wanted two of his greatest loves to have the same name. She decided then and there maybe it was time to back off on her criticism of his deal with Shirley. She could see she was creating conflict that he didn't need right now.

Monday morning they managed to get everything and everybody aboard for the trip. They gave Jake a pill to quiet him down a little, and gave Timmy his medication for the same reason. Timmy loved to fly but he could get impatient, and he didn't like all the belts and harnesses. The last thing Arnie found room for was a case of his homemade beer for Julie's dad, packing it carefully so it wouldn't break if they hit a little turbulence.

The flight itself would take about two hours, and Arnie had filed a flight plan with the local airport, giving his destination as Thunder Bay, Canada. Because it involved crossing an international border, the Canadians also had been notified. His course would be one straight line from home to Thunder Bay.

When the plane was loaded, Arnie leaned over, and with what Julie always called his trademark shit-eating grin, kissed her softly. He set the throttle for takeoff. They taxied straight out from the dock and were up and away. Just like that.

Timmy went to sleep almost immediately, and Jake was whimpering but behaving himself. Julie slipped her fingers through the slots in the side of his pet carrier, rubbing his cold wet nose and scratching his ears.

It was warm in the plane despite a chill in the air outside. They had brought warm jackets because it could get nasty in Thunder Bay in the middle of September. Arnie popped a CD of Tanya Tucker into the disk player, set the automatic pilot, and massaged Julie's neck as she tried to relax. She too was asleep within minutes.

He marveled at the responsiveness of his new plane. He couldn't stop feeling the soft leather upholstery and turning things on and off just to see them work again. The old plane had been simple and had only the bare essentials. This plane was built for comfort as well, and what the hell, he deserved it.

All day the weather bureau at Minneapolis International Airport had been tracking a developing low pressure system that had formed over southern Minnesota and was pressing its way north. It was expected to stay south of Arnie's flight path, so no mention had been made of it when he had called in at takeoff. But the high-pressure system they were in was collapsing rapidly, and the extremely powerful low was rushing north with a speed no one thought possible. To top it off, it was combining with a northeastern low coming in off Lake Superior. The Duluth weather bureau was now predicting some major instability for small aircraft.

Arnie had seen the clouds and they puzzled him, but not wanting to alarm Julie, he did not arouse her from her nap. He also elected not to call Duluth for a weather update. He just figured he would fly straight north for a while to avoid any trouble, and then head east when he was around it.

There was some lightning off to his right, and a few raindrops were hitting the windshield, but otherwise it was not that bad. Nothing he hadn't handled before. The wipers whisked softly on the windshield. The storm clouds didn't seem to be that high, and if he hadn't had the family along he would have just gone over them. It could get cold at higher altitudes and high altitude flying could also bring some problems with wind currents he didn't need right now, and this plane was too new for him to experiment. He slipped the disk from the CD player and took another from its case and put it in, but for the moment he didn't push play. He needed to concentrate on his flying for a few minutes.

In ten minutes he was far off the course he had filed with the airport, but he could see the back edge of the storm, so he wasn't going to call them about his location, he would just have to call again in a few minutes when he made the correction to get back on track. It had gotten quite dark, so he switched on the cockpit lights, which also illuminated the instrument panel better, to check his heading. He disconnected the automatic pilot and was flying manually again.

Arnie was right on the edge of the storm. Another ten miles to the west would have been more comfortable, but he was just about around it. It could chase him if it wanted to. *"We're too fast for that storm,"* he thought to himself, but just for the hell of it he gave the throttle another notch and heard the engine's drone change pitch.

Two things Arnie had taken for granted were going to be trouble for him in a few minutes. Number one was his assumption that the Duluth Airport had him on radar and they knew where he was. Number two was that he was far enough away from the storm to be safe.

It was making him nervous enough to open up a pouch of Beechnut, though, and stuff a wad in his cheek. His empty coffee cup became his spit cup.

The first bolt of lightning woke Julie. It was like a flashbulb had gone off in her face. "Arnie," she said, startled. "What's happening?"

"Nothing to worry about, Julie babe. A little storm came up from somewhere, but we are nearly around it. Just relax." He reached over and massaged her neck some and spit in his cup.

"Ish," Julie said and leaned against the door, her signal that she hated his chewing.

The second bolt of lightning hit the plane's tail like an explosion, blowing off a piece of the vertical stabilizer and taking out the entire electrical system. The plane was swerving wildly, and Arnie fought with the controls to get it settled down. They were losing altitude fast. He knew by looking at the horizon, not the altimeter, because they had no altimeter. They had no instruments at all, nor did they have an engine. Arnie keyed the mike and tried in vain, but the radio was dead, and so would they be if he didn't do something fast. He managed to stabilize the plane enough that he was flying straight and the vibrations had gone away. Something was still drastically wrong with the controls and the electrical system and the way they were losing altitude, he had better figure it out in a hurry. A quick look behind him showed the damage to the tail. A large piece of it was missing.

Julie was terrified, and slid down in her seat with a low mournful cry. She had seen a look on Arnie's face that she knew signaled he was in some kind of trouble. This was the exact reason she had hated flying. She just knew something like this would happen someday.

Timmy woke up and started crying and Jake was scratching at the side of his carrier. He wanted out, and Arnie wanted out too. Out of the mess they were in. His mind was swarming with thoughts and he tried to calm himself down. He had dead sticked planes in before and he could do it again if there was a place to land. He had floats and there was a lot of water down there. There would be no land down there that wasn't full of trees.

The plane was very hard to control horizontally and it seemed nose heavy despite the adjustments he made with the flaps. Arnie turned nearly 180 degrees back into the storm to keep the wind straight at them for control and to slow the aircraft. That same wind was now on them with a vengeance, buffeting the aircraft. Rain was pelting the windshield, and visibility, with no wipers, was all but nonexistent.

For Arnie there was only one solution. Find a lake and set it down if he could. The area they were over was roughly fifty percent water, so Arnie scanned the ground for signs of a lake. With no altimeter he had no way of knowing how high he was. The alarm system that should tell him when he was too low was also gone, and there was a smell of burnt wiring in the plane. The smoke set off an alarm in Jake's mind and now he was barking and scraping furiously at the sides of his carrier.

The one thing Arnie could feel was that they were descending, and sooner or later they would run out of airspace. That was a given. He grabbed for the radio mic once more but it was still dead. He dropped it to the floor.

Julie was praying with her head hung, not making any sound but soft sobbing. Timmy was wailing, but Arnie wasn't hearing or seeing anything except what was in front of him. He had tuned the rest of them out. Tobacco juice was running out of the corner of his mouth, and he spit the whole wad on the floor before he choked.

The trees appeared before he could react, and then he saw water. He pulled the nose up as far as he could and cut the dead throttle out of habit. They were about thirty feet over the water, and Arnie felt they had made it. The plane was settling down, her floats outstretched like a duck skidding in on a farmland pond. Even Julie seemed to catch a glimmer of hope as she saw the water coming at them.

There was nothing else Arnie could do but hang on. The plane was where he wanted it and was level enough. If only the lake was long enough, he could see nothing in the foggy conditions. He reached for Julie's shoulder, and with a sudden glimpse of land and forest they hit the tree nose-first about twenty feet off the ground.

It was an old Norway white pine about a hundred years old. It had seen a lot of things, in its life, but it had never been blasted by a Cessna Skyhawk before. It shook to the bottom of its roots and bent over at least ten feet in a backward bow, but it didn't break. It took the blow like an offensive lineman being nailed by the noseguard, and then retaliated by standing back up and bowing the other way before standing still. The front of the plane was stuck to the tree, impaled on an old dead limb, but the tail fell abruptly to the ground. The plane hung there at a forty-five degree angle, its nose in the tree, its tail buried in the wet earth.

The emergency transponder on the tail was silent. Steam was coming from the engine compartment, but no smoke. With luck there would be no fire.

When they had hit, Julie's right arm had been thrust up to the cabin ceiling and the same limb they had impaled themselves on had come through the windshield and passed under her right arm, ripping her shirt and part of her bra from her body. It also took a large piece of flesh from under her arm and most of the skin off the side of her breast, the worst was a wood sliver from the branch, driven deep into her armpit.

The end of the branch had passed over Timmy's head behind Julie. Had he not been thrust forward against the harness by the impact, so his head was down, it would have hit him directly in the face. Timmy was not injured, but he could not raise his head because he was under the limb. Jake had slammed against the front of his pet carrier that had rammed into the back of Arnie's seat when the belt broke. He was bruised and yelping but seemed fine otherwise.

Arnie felt nothing. The corner of Jake's pet carrier had driven forward into the back of his seat and broken his back, four vertebrae above his tailbone. The pain had been there for an instant, and then there was nothing, no feeling at all in his body below his arms. His shoulder harness saved him from any other injuries, but he was badly hurt and unconscious.

The pain at first was more than Julie could bear, and she screamed out loud. Her right arm was still pinned against the ceiling of the plane, and her side throbbed angrily. Rain was coming in the broken windshield and soaking her, but it also washed away some of the pain. She could hear Timmy crying and Jake yelping, but Arnie was silent, and she turned as far as she could to look at him. The branch had her almost sideways in her seat with her back to him. Her neck hurt to turn it this far, but it was the only way she could see Arnie. His head was hung down, but she could see his chest going up and down. He was breathing.

She turned her attention back to herself. She needed to get her arm back where it belonged and off this damn branch that had ripped half her clothes off. It was light enough that she could see the road rash on her breast and the sliver sticking out of her armpit. She had to get that sliver out first or she would never be able to lower her arm.

Julie reached over with her left hand and grabbed the sliver. She held it between her thumb and forefinger until she got a firm grip. "Dear Jesus, help me!" she screamed as she yanked, but it only came out partway. Blood was running down her side. It was now or never, because she was going to faint. With a scream that echoed through the forest, she pulled it out the rest of the way.

She passed out momentarily, and when she came to, was confused as to where she was. Then reality hit. The sliver was still in her hand and she held it up and looked at it. It was six inches long and about one-half inch in diameter coming almost to a point, and some of her tissue was hanging from the end. The wound was oozing blood but not spurting, so that was good. Julie took a pile of tissues that was in a box between the seats and rolled it into a ball. She shoved it under her arm while pulling her arm loose from over the branch.

For a few minutes she could only cry and shake uncontrollably. She had never hurt this bad before, but at the same time she realized that right now she was the only one capable of doing anything. She checked on Arnie again now that she was straight in her seat, but there was no change. He was unconscious, his breathing coming in a snoring rasp. Tobacco juice was still oozing out of the corner of his mouth as his head hung forward, his body still restrained by the shoulder harness. Julie pushed his eyelid open with her finger but his eyes appeared to be rolled back in his head.

"Timmy." Julie said his name out loud as she turned as much in the seat as she could to see him. She remembered catching a glimpse of him under the branch when he was crying but she hadn't heard a sound from him since. She was 180 degrees turned around then, and now looking between the seats she could see him. She reached around the seat, felt Timmy's head, and touched his tear-stained face. He was still crying softly, but almost to himself, he stopped long enough to say, "Mommy, I'm afraid." He rarely called her that, let alone spoke at all, and she recognized the fear in his voice.

"Timmy, don't cry, sweetheart. Mommy's going to get us out of here in a minute." She massaged his chest. "Do you have any owies, Timmy?" He didn't answer her, but he seemed to be calm enough. She felt his legs and they seemed fine. Julie stuck her fingers through Jake's cage and he licked them.

The plane sitting at a forty-five degree angle made moving around difficult, that, and there was also that damn branch in her face. Julie unhooked all of her belts and crawled partway between the seats to get an even closer look at Timmy. *Oh my God, how it hurt to move her arm and shoulder,* she had to stop for a second or she was going to faint again. Timmy seemed to be fine and had settled down quite a bit.

She made her way back up into her seat and got the door opened a little before it jammed. It looked to be about ten feet to the ground. Julie looked back at Arnie again, and just as quickly as she had settled down, she came unglued. "Goddamn you, Arnie," she screamed. "You and your fucking plane. I told you we would crash someday, didn't I? But you had all the answers. Well, what's the answer now, Arnie? You're half-dead and this goddamn branch tore half my tit off ... and ... and ... What am I going to do?" She collapsed with her head in her lap, sobbing once again.

Arnie moaned and raised his head and Julie stared at him, suddenly stopping her sobbing. "Arnie, wake up," she said. "Arnie, wake up and help me. Arnie I'm sorry sweetheart. I didn't mean to say what I said. It's just that it hurts so much and I have no idea where we are or how to get out of here. Wait till you see this hole in my armpit. Arnie?"

"Julie, I can't move. My legs are numb and my back is killing me. Help me, Julie."

She stared at him. What was he saying? That he was hurt too? "What hurts Arnie? Where?"

He didn't answer her but appeared to pass out again. When Arnie came to the second time he told her he could not feel the lower half of his body.

Julie came to the conclusion that Arnie was paralyzed from the chest down. He regained full consciousness and almost seemed to take over. "You need to get down to the ground Julie and find out where we are. You should also try to get Timmy and Jake out of the plane."

Julie stared at him. "Sure, Arnie, I'll get right at that," she said sarcastically, and then started crying again.

The rain had stopped and the sun was shining brightly by this time. Julie's arm still hurt badly, and she was having trouble stopping the bleeding in her armpit. Her bra had been torn in half and her breast was so sore that the thought of putting it back on made her cringe, so she took the other half off too. She buttoned up her shirt for now. She would look at things later. She had to keep her arm down to her side to hold the tissues in the armpit, but that was all right. It hurt too damn much to move anyway.

By putting her feet against the door, she was able to get it open the rest of the way. She sat on the floor with her feet dangling out, looking at the ground below. If she got out, how was she ever going to get back up here? She started to cry again. "I just knew it would come to this someday," she sobbed.

She could hear water. Waves were breaking on land, but all she could see was the pine forest. There were tin and glass shards below the plane as well as a lot of pine needles that might cushion her fall. "If I jump and break my leg, Arnie, then what are we going to do?" She blubbered. Finally she resolved there was nothing she could do but jump and she did, landing on her feet and nearly passing out from the pain in her arm and breast. The only way she could stand the pain was to walk holding her elbow in her hand. She needed to make a sling somehow. Maybe her discarded bra would work. If it couldn't hold her boob maybe it could hold something like her elbow. She would have laughed at the thought if she wasn't in so much pain.

She sat under the plane for a while, and then got up and walked toward the sound of the waves. On the shore she was looking at about five hundred feet of open water, and more land on the other side.

Timmy was crying again so she went back to the plane. The right wing had broken off and was laying about thirty feet away in the woods. It was still in one piece. Maybe she could shove it in the open door and use it for a ramp to get back up in the plane. Julie was amazed at how light it was, and she was able to maneuver it into place using only her good arm. Putting her feet in the flaps on the back of the wing, she crawled back inside the plane. She got Timmy in the front seat with her, and after checking him over more closely and finding nothing wrong, she had him slide down the wing, which he seemed to think was great fun. She also managed to get Jake's cage open. He came out licking her face, and she pushed him down the wing.

Arnie was in and out of it. One minute he made sense, and the next minute he was muttering about his poor plane and how his back hurt. Julie looked him over more closely, and although one of his ankles looked broken, she couldn't find anything else wrong with him. There was a bulge in his back she could feel while sliding her hand between his back and the seat. "Just a broken back and ankle, Arnie," she muttered sarcastically. "I can't get you out of your seat, and you can't move yourself, so you are just going to have to stay put in your damn plane." And then she started crying again, her head in Arnie's lap. "I'm sorry, Arnie, but I don't know what the hell to do."

CHAPTER 5

▼

She had only been with Arnie for a few minuets when suddenly she remembered that Timmy was all alone down below. She jerked her head up to look around and saw him under the plane, piling up dead pine needles into a big pile. She didn't know where Jake was so she whistled, and he came bursting out of the brush, looking for whoever had called him. Finding only Timmy, he went over and licked his face.

Sliding down the wing to the ground again, Julie sat down and pulled Timmy into her lap. "Are you having fun sweetheart?" she asked him. Timmy just looked at her and then went to get more needles for his pile. At first their plight had seemed so desperate, but now she was settling down a little. They were all alive and in no immediate danger, and it had to be only a matter of time before someone came looking for them. She took the corner of her shirt and spit washed Timmy's face. "You are doing such a good job for me." Timmy smiled and went back to his chore.

It was getting late in the day and no one had come for them yet, so Julie guessed that maybe they would have to spend the night. Maybe she should think about some kind of shelter outside. It was going to be damn uncomfortable in the plane; she knew that. She was getting hungry, and she wondered about Timmy. He had to be hungry too.

Climbing back in the plane, Julie dug through the treats she had packed and found some Ritz Crackers and cheese. There wasn't a lot of food in the plane but they wouldn't be here long.

She needed a knife to cut the cheese but had forgotten to pack one. *Wait! Arnie had his knife in his pocket. He always carried it.* "Arnie, are you awake?" Julie asked.

Arnie moaned some kind of an answer that was unintelligible, so she crawled to where she could see his face. "Arnie, I need your knife. Are you hungry? I thought I would cut some cheese to go with these crackers. We need to eat something, don't we? How long will it take for them to come and get us?"

Arnie just stared at Julie. His head was getting clearer now and he could think a little. "Julie, I am so sorry," he finally said. Tears ran down his face and dripped on his chest.

"Arnie, don't cry," Julie said. "If you bawl I'm going to start bawling again too, and we'll get nowhere with that." She had never seen Arnie cry before and it unnerved her.

"Where are you hurt?" he asked. Julie showed him the hole under her arm and her bruised and scraped breast. "There's a first aid kit under my seat," he said. "Put some ointment and gauze on that before you get an infection. Where's Timmy?"

"Down below" Julie answered. "He's fine."

"Jake?"

"He's fine too."

Arnie had no idea when anybody would find them or if the transponder was even working. There was no signal on his cell phone either, but he didn't expect one in this area. They agreed that Julie would make some kind of shelter under the plane for her, Timmy, and the dog. There was a tarp in the plane that was used for covering the airplane cabin when it was parked outside, and she would use that. She needed to make a big fire as that might draw some attention, and they could use the warmth. Arnie thought it would be safe enough for them to drink out of the lake. He was very thirsty.

Julie gave up on the cheese for the moment and climbed down with Arnie's coffee cup to get him some water. She stopped long enough to explain to Timmy that she needed him to gather sticks, and she showed him what she needed.

"You make me a pile of sticks this big," Julie said, holding her hands at waist level. "We are going to have a nice campfire just like the ones we have at home." The mention of home stuck a familiar word to Timmy, and he got a far away look in his eye staring at the lake for a minute with a stick in his hand. Julie realized the connection and rumpled his hair to change the subject. He seemed to be confused right now but not really traumatized by the events that had taken place. She would have to keep an eye on him though, or he might wander off.

Jake came back soaking wet as he had gone swimming or duck chasing. Something he was famous for.

It was fifty yards or so to the lake and carrying the first aid kit, Julie took off her shirt to wash the injured area of her chest. The water was so cold it made her gasp, and it hurt so much to touch her injuiries that it took her breath away. She let her bruised skin dry and then smeared first aid cream over the area. She made a pad for the injured side of her breast, but instead of tape, she put it in the cup of her bra and put that back on after fixing the broken straps. She had given up on the sling idea. Then she moved down the beach a little for cleaner water and reached out into the lake, rinsing and filling the coffee cup.

When Julie got back to the plane, Timmy had a brush pile three feet high. She told him what a good job he was doing and climbed back up to Arnie. It was tricky trying to climb up that slippery wing without spilling the water, but she did remarkably well.

Arnie drank all of the water and laid his head back. "Whatever happens, Julie, we have to stay with the plane."

Julie nodded her head. "Can I have your knife?"

"Only if you will help me go to the bathroom without wetting all over myself and give me my chew," he said.

Arnie was able to move his right arm and hand and his left hand. He could not raise his left arm but he could open and close his hand. Julie fashioned a funnel out of a paper towel roll, and Arnie was able to pee into it without getting himself wet, letting his urine run out the half opened door.. The fact that he had bladder function was encouraging to her. When he had finished she found his tobacco and gave it to him, and made him take a couple aspirins that she had in her purse.

Arnie could not reach into his pocket himself, so Julie dug around and found his knife and a lighter he carried. There was also a little box in his pocket that caught her curiosity, but she never bothered to take it out and soon forgot about it.

Back on the ground once more, Julie saw that Timmy had piled all of the brush under the plane so she moved it over and got some pine needles burning and started a fire. It would be dark before long, so she went back to the plane and found their coats and one blanket. She draped Arnie's coat around his shoulders and did what she could to make him comfortable before she went back down. He didn't want anything to eat.

Julie put Timmy's coat on him and made him lie by the fire, his head in her lap. They had cheese and crackers, split a Baby Ruth candy bar and drank lake water. "Should I tell you a story like we did at—?" She stopped herself from finishing the sentence but Timmy did not seem to notice. The light from the campfire was mirrored in his moist eyes as he watched the flames. He nodded his head yes to her unfinished question, but his eyes were already closing.

Jake looked on with hungry eyes while they ate, but he seemed to understand that he was going to have to fend for himself, there would be no handouts, so he curled up and went to sleep next to Timmy. Off to the east, it looked like more rain was coming.

By 3:30 p.m. Julie's parents had been at the airport for over three hours, and there was still no sign of Arnie and Julie. Her father, Tom, called their cell phone but got the message center, so he called the airport where Arnie would have filed a flight plan. Irv Engstrom, a friend of Arnie's, was on duty and said that they had indeed filed a flight plan. In fact, he had talked to Arnie just prior to takeoff. He said he would drive out to Arnie's place and take a look, and then get back to them at the airport in Thunder Bay.

It was four o'clock before Irv got out to Arnie and Julie's and nothing seemed out of place. The old Piper was still there, pulled up on shore now, and when Irv first saw it, he had thought, "Shit, they're still here." But then he remembered Arnie talking about the new plane, and he went up to the house and looked around. The door was locked and there was a note on the door to please use the back door, but that was locked too. Irv had been here many times and Jake would always be there to greet him before he could get out of the car, but now he was nowhere to be seen.

He walked down to the dock and looked out over the lake, wondering about what he had seen. They had to have gone on that trip Arnie talked about. There was no other explanation for them not being there. What had been curiosity was now turning into serious concern, and Irv called the Thunder Bay Airport from his car. He did not ask for Tom at first, but asked for the traffic controller and explained the situation. Yes, they had received a flight plan that called for BR1072, Arnie's call number, to arrive in the area at about one p.m. They hadn't heard from him and had seen no sign of him arriving. His plane was late, but they didn't seem concerned about them because a lot of float planes elected to land at some lake instead of the airport and never bothered to tell them.

Irv had Tom paged at the airport and told him what he had discovered. He also told him that even if they had problems, Arnie was a good pilot with a state-of-the-art aircraft with floats, and that most likely he had just landed on a lake somewhere. Still, he was going to call the Civil Air Patrol, and they would start a search as soon as possible. He placed another call to the airport at Duluth to see if they would help with a search. They said they would do something in the morning.

Julie's parents were visibly upset. Despite Irv's talk about them setting down someplace else, they felt something bad had happened. They left the airport with friends that had come to the airport with them and went home.

Irv went to the hanger as soon as he got back and had his plane prepared for flight. Tom Nestels, another friend of Arnie's agreed to ride along as a second pair of eyes, and they set off on their search. They flew out to Arnie's home, and set the same course Arnie would have taken, heading northeast. It would be dark in a couple of hours, but they would search until then. If they didn't see anything, they'd organize a bigger search in the morning.

The rain came again, but it was a soft rain with no wind and lasted for only an hour or so. Julie crawled up to check on Arnie once more before dark, but he was sleeping, so she just sat and looked at him for a few minutes. It was hard to imagine this big rugged man rendered so helpless. In the morning she was going to check him over for any other injuries and see if she could determine just how badly he was hurt. While she was in the plane away from Timmy, she changed the dressing under her arm once more. The gauze was cleaner and most of the bleeding had stopped. She couldn't bend her head to clearly see how deep the wound was, so she just had to judge by feel more than anything else. She still had a lot of pain when she moved her arm, so she tried to keep it as still as possible.

Timmy was sleeping with his head resting on Jake when she got down. Poor Jake, Julie hoped he would find some food tomorrow, and maybe he would find something for them too. *How were they going to eat if nobody came soon to rescue them? She wondered, and thought Arnie's fishing rod!* She had seen it in the back of the plane. *She would catch a fish and cook it, but in what?* It had been a long day, and while Julie thought about what she was going to use to fry a fish she hadn't caught yet, sleep caught up with her.

It was a rugged night. Timmy woke up several times. He was getting over his initial confusion, but now he was hungry and cold, and had no concept of how much trouble they were in. He couldn't figure out why they didn't just leave and go home where it was warm and there was a lot to eat. Julie had managed to stay fairly comfortable herself, using Jake's rump for a pillow. If only his belly hadn't been so noisy.

When Julie woke up, Jake was gone and Timmy was sitting up and staring at her. She found some more wood and got the fire going so they could warm up.

She gave Timmy some more crackers, and climbed up to see how Arnie had come through the night using her stiff sore arm as little as necessary.

Arnie was awake and seemed in better spirits than he had been the night before. He had regained some of the movement in his left arm, so that encouraged both of them. Julie helped him position himself so he could pee once more, and then went down to get him some more water, but this time she also brought down the suitcase she had packed. In it were clean clothes and she wanted to change her and Timmy's underwear. There was no reason they couldn't try to be clean.

The sun was shining brightly and by ten it had warmed up considerably. After helping Arnie get comfortable again, Julie went back to the lake with Timmy and they sat side by side on a rock a few feet from shore, while she washed both of them and got them into fresh clothes. She washed her injured chest carefully, and put some more ointment on it. Her breast was healing fine, but the hole under her arm was red and inflamed, and she was worried about infection. It looked like a blood clot had formed over the hole, and she thought about removing it but was just too squeamish for that right now. She looked in the first aid kit once more for any other creams or salves, but there was only the one tube.

Back at the crash site a final search of the rest of the plane did net her a few surprises that might help them. She found a flare gun, Arnie's case of homemade beer with only one bottle broken, and a twelve pack of Coke. She also found some rope and another tarp that would make a better tent then the one they had been using. Except for the beer, she took everything else down to the ground and covered it up under the plane in case they needed it.

The only planes they had heard since yesterday were high-flying commercial jets, but Arnie said that maybe if their transponder was working the jets would pick it up. They were in a restricted area where no one was supposed to fly below five thousand feet, but they didn't know that, as they had no idea where they were. Arnie didn't think they had come this far west. He had gotten a map from the pocket in the door and was looking at it when Julie came back up to talk.

"Julie, I want you to take a walk," he said. "Some of these lakes have campers that come in canoes. Look for smoke from campfires or people paddling across the lake. Maybe if you can tell me what the lake looks like, I can figure out where we are on this map. None of these lakes are identical in shape."

Julie looked at Arnie and said. "What about Timmy and Jake?"

"You can bring Timmy back up here and strap him in his seat and I'll take care of him. Take Jake with you."

When she went back down, Timmy was sleeping and Jake was eating a rotten fish he had found. *Another day without food, dog, and we both will be eating rotten fish,* she thought. Speaking of fish, she still had Arnie's rod and reel. Maybe before she went walking she would try her luck.

Irv and Tom Nestels had seen nothing yesterday and they had returned to the airport and called the Duluth airport. A full-scale search would start today by the Civil Air Patrol and other planes from Duluth. The search would be coordinated by the Duluth Air Base, which had a lot of experience in searches. Arnie's friends at the Duluth Airport would also assist, as would Irv and a couple of other pilots from town.

The news of Arnie's disappearance was prominent on the front page news in the morning paper, and Shirley Capes spent the day on the phone enlisting more people to participate in the search. Shirley was heartbroken and worried. Arnie was not only a very important part of her newspaper; he was also a good friend. She thought about the plane and how happy he had seemed when he first saw it, running his hands over the metal and staring in the open door like he was afraid to touch anything. She thought about his concern for his writing freedom and how maybe she had gone too far in her dealings. She hoped there was no animosity.

The ashtray on her desk was overflowing with butts, and a smoky cloud hung over the room. It was not like Shirley to feel this helpless, she was always on top of her game, but right now she didn't know what to do except light up.

Julie fished for about an hour and managed to get three perch, weighing about six ounces each. She cleaned them and roasted them on a stick over the fire. They were delicious, and she, Timmy and Jake each ate one, along with a few more crackers and a can of Coke. The meager meal bolstered Julie's mood and confidence a bit. Arnie still refused any food.

Julie finally worked up the energy to go for that walk, and she put Timmy back in the plane after giving him some of the medicine she had brought to mellow him out. She walked back down to the shoreline with Jake bounding along in front of her. This incident was like a dream come true for him. He loved to be in the woods and explore. The shoreline seemed to curve away from her; both to the left and right, and the lake became much wider as she walked away. She must be on a peninsula, or the lake was shaped like an hourglass and they were at the narrow point. Finally after much thought, she elected to go to her right.

Her energy level was down again, and Julie felt like she might have a fever. Putting her hand on her forehead didn't tell her much, but if there was a hot spot it was under her arm. Maybe when she got back she would have Arnie look at it, because it was just too hard for her to see. The pain in her arm had moved down into her hand now, and she noticed that her fingers were pretty swollen.

But she had to put that aside for now and try to figure out where they were. Arnie had given Julie a pad and paper, asking her to take some notes and try to draw the contour of the shoreline if she could get high enough to see more than just a few feet ahead of her. For the most part the brush grew right down to the water's edge, and sometimes it was easier to just walk in the water at the edge of the lake. The water was so cold, though, that she had to get out from time to time just to warm up her feet. She took off her stockings and left only her tennis shoes on to cushion her feet from the rocks.

The shoreline seemed to keep dropping away, and the lake was a lot wider here. It looked now like it was about a mile across and the wind blowing across it was pushing up enough waves that she had to retreat back to shore, as she was getting her jeans wet. It still seemed like she was walking in a circle, but it was hard to tell because the woods were so thick.

Soon it seemed like the lake was getting narrower again. She had seen no sign of anybody or anything, except a few squirrels and a porcupine that Jake nearly got into it with. That's all she needed right now she thought, a dog full of quills.

She stopped to rest on a log for a few minutes. The walking had awakened her bowels and she needed to do something about that. She sat on the log with her butt hanging over it and relieved herself, noting that she had gotten diarrhea from something. *Must be the lake water*, she thought. She waddled to the water's edge with her pants down and washed herself off, as she had made a mess of things. Then turning around to pull her pants up, she glanced into the woods and saw the white airplane propped up against the tree.

They were on an island. She'd been walking in a circle. Julie sat on the ground and started crying. She tossed the paper and pencil Arnie had given her on the ground and stomped on them screaming with frustration. "Damn you, Arnie," she sobbed. "You crashed us on an island. You had the whole wilderness to crash this plane in, and you had to pick a goddamn island. Now what are we going to do, Arnie? Just what in the name of God are we going to do on this fucking island? We are just like the goddamn Swiss Family Robertson, or whatever their name was."

She cried softly for a while before realizing what a futile action her fit of anger was. She sat up and looked at the plane again with her tearstained face, and hiccupped softly. She needed to be strong. Nobody else here was going to help them. Jake cocked his head to one side and looked at her as if he couldn't figure out what the problem was. Julie grabbed the big dog by the ears and kissed his muzzle, wiping her face in his soft coat, and Jake licked her tears away with a look of real concern.

She dug the pencil and paper out of the dirt, and drew a circle. "That's the picture, Arnie," she said, and then another wave of diarrhea hit her.

CHAPTER 6

▼

On Tuesday morning the Civil Air Patrol met at the Duluth office to go over preparations for a search starting at Sunrise Lake, Minnesota, and continuing on to Thunder Bay Ontario, to find flight BR1072. The flight had taken off from Sunrise Lake yesterday morning, and no trace had been found or heard of them since.

There had been a storm in the area, but it was believed to be behind the area they were flying into, and shouldn't have affected them if they followed their flight plan. Radio contact with the airport outside of Sunrise Lake had been made at eight a.m. on Monday morning, announcing that they were taking off. The plane was a Cessna Skyhawk, white with blue stripes and blue designs on it, and was equipped with floats for water landing. It was believed to be carrying the pilot and his family. There was also a report that the plane was new to the pilot and he night not have been familiar with all of the instruments, but in the next breath the report also talked about his years of flying experience. It was the usual speculation that always accompanied incidents like this.

A large map of the wilderness area was spread out on the table, and several pilots were standing around it while the head of the Civil Air Patrol showed each of them the grid on the map that they would cover. The Coast Guard had sent a communications aircraft up early this morning to listen for the transponder on the plane, but they hadn't had a report back from them yet.

The morning newspaper gave front-page coverage to the story. It stated that Arnie Bottelmiller, a well-known columnist and outdoor advocate, along with his family, was missing on a flight over the wilderness area. It went on to say that a full-scale search of the area was underway by the Coast Guard and the Civil Air

Patrol. Shirley Capes, the editor of the paper and a reported long time friend of Arnie's, had been interviewed on Channel Four Television, but she became too distraught and they had to stop the interview.

Back in the small bank where Julie worked, a bouquet of flowers sat on her desk, along with good wishes and prayers from friends and colleagues. The mood in the bank was subdued and worried. Julie was very well liked and an important member of their small organization. Most of her co-workers seemed too upset to talk to reporters, but Stan Iverson, the bank President gave a short statement and talked about Julie's work and how well liked and admired she was and how concerned they all were.

At Sunrise Lake, Arnie's mother was staying in the house. She sat in the porch looking out over the lake for any sign of her son and his family. The ashtray beside her was stuffed with cigarette butts, and her hands were shaking around the coffee cup she held to warm them. A deeply devout woman, she preferred to pray and keep to herself.

Julie went back to the plane, but just sat on the ground under it for a while. She was too upset to talk with Arnie at the moment, and she was feeling sick to her stomach. Jake curled up on her feet. It was quiet above her, and she needed to think before she talked to Arnie again. They were in serious trouble, as far as she was concerned. Her fever was not getting better, and the whole right side of her chest felt like it was on fire. Diarrhea was racking her insides and she had cramps that would come in waves, even though there was nothing left inside her. Timmy was also a big concern, especially if she got any sicker and was unable to take care of him. They needed to think this out, and soon.

Arnie knew, too, that things looked grim. Although his body was paralyzed from his chest down, his mind was clear. If the transponder was working, they would have been found by now. He could see it from where he was sitting and it appeared to be fine from the outside, but unbeknownst to him, the lightning had destroyed the entire electrical system in the aircraft. There was no sign of power to anything. The transponder had its own battery backup, but had that also been burned out? He just didn't know.

He heard Julie return and wondered what she was doing down there, so he finally called out to her. She hadn't been gone very long, that was for sure.

"Hi honey," Julie said as she stuck her head back in the airplane door and slid into her seat. The anger she had experienced a few minutes ago had subsided, and she needed to talk, rationally. "Arnie, we're on an island," she said, looking at his sad, concerned face. Her eyes started to well up with tears and she fought the emotions back. She had to stay strong, which was a switch for her and Arnie.

"I wondered why you were back so soon." He picked up his map and studied it some more. The small round island they were on was on the south end of the lake. There were only two lakes that fit that profile on the map. "Julie, we're either on Sand Point Lake, or Kato Lake," he said.

"I am so happy for us," she said sarcastically.

"No, Julie, listen. If we know where we are, then I can figure out how you can walk out of here. If they can't find us, we are going to have to do something to help ourselves."

Julie sat quietly for a second, and then said, "Arnie, I need to rest for a while. I've got an infection in my chest. I'm shiting every five minutes, I have a fever, and I'm thirsty and hungry. That's just the good news." A few tears slid down her face and she sniffed her nose and wiped it on her sleeve.

Arnie reached over and stroked her hair. "Let's work together," he said.

She put her head on his shoulder, and they sat like that until Timmy's whimpering brought them both back to reality.

"You stink, Arnie Bottelmiller," she said sitting up. "You need a bath." It was as if she had just gotten her second wind and her mood changed dramatically.

Julie unbuckled Timmy and helped him down the wing to the ground and gave him part of a can of Coke she had opened. She asked Timmy to gather more brush and pine needles for a big fire and told him that she would be right back.

When she went back up to Arnie, she brought water in an old hard hat that she found in the survival gear. She washed his face first and then took his shirt off and washed his chest and underarms. Putting her hands as far as she could around his back without moving him, she could feel the misaligned bones in his spine. As far as she could see, that and his broken ankle were his only injuries.

She unbuckled his pants and ran her hands around his hips and groin area, but everything felt fine, at least as far as she could tell. Arnie didn't seem to notice anything she did to him below the waist. She left his pants unbuckled; it would be easier for him to relieve himself that way. She felt the small flat box in his pocket for the second time as she rearranged his pants, and this time she slid her hand in his pocket and took it out.

There was no mistaking what it looked like. Arnie was still looking at his map and paid little or no attention to what she was doing. "Arnie, what is this?" she asked without opening the box.

For a moment he was caught off guard, but at last he said, "Open it, sweetheart. It's for you."

Julie's hands were shaking as she opened the lid and looked at the white gold ring with a large diamond in the middle and two-smaller ones on each side. Also in the box was a matching wedding band. Inside the wedding ring was engraved. ***To my eternal love.***

She was crying again, but this time they were tears of joy. "Oh, Arnie," was all she could say.

"I wanted to surprise you at your folk's place. I thought we could set a date and make all of the plans."

"Let's set a date right now, Arnie."

Arnie slapped at his shirt pocket. "I don't have my calendar with me."

Julie's tears turned to laughter and they hugged. They held each other for a few moments and discussed their situation. They would wait until Friday night, and if nobody had found them by then, and if Julie felt better, she would have to find her way out of the area. She would need to take Timmy with her, because Arnie wouldn't be able to care for him. It certainly wouldn't be easy, but it could be done. Arnie would give her a crash course on survival, and he would give her a map to go by.

There was a definite difference between Sand Point and Kato Lake and Julie was going to have to do some investigating before he could finish the map. Sand Point was the closest to civilization, but Arnie had a gut feeling that they were on Kato. They couldn't have been that far south yet as they were in the air for over an hour when the lightening hit them. On the opposite end of the lake there would be a river flowing in on Kato, and Julie was going to have to walk around the lake to see if it was there. She would have to swim to shore, as they were on an island, and then she would have to swim back to get Timmy and Jake before she left.

But not today, today she would rest and get better. She had momentarily forgotten about Timmy, and now she quickly looked below and saw that he had another pile of brush ready for her. She kissed Arnie and slid down the wing.

It was getting dark so she lit the fire, and then she and Timmy went down to the lake to try casting for fish once more. On the second cast Julie got a nice walleye, probably close to three pounds. She was so excited that she ran back to the plane and hollered at Arnie to look out the window and see what she had caught. Arnie laughed and said, "Let's eat woman."

This time, instead of roasting it over the fire on a stick, Julie laid the meat in the aluminum hard hat she had found in the plane and fried it. They had never eaten better fish ... walleyed pike fried in Arnie's helmet with just a touch of hair oil. After she had fed Arnie and Timmy, Julie ate the rest and let Jake lick out the helmet. Poor Jake, he would have to start hunting soon if he was going to survive. Julie, Timmy and Jake curled up by the fire on their tarp and went to sleep. Her chest felt a little better, and she hadn't had diarrhea in two hours. Things were looking up.

The next morning they woke to a drizzle, so they got back in the plane to wait it out. Jake sat down under the plane and whimpered because he couldn't get up the wing and didn't want to be left alone in the rain.

The weather gave Julie and Arnie time to finish their plans. Julie would fish and get stronger today, and in the morning she would swim to the opposite shore and walk around the lake. With what she discovered, Arnie could finish the map on Thursday. On Friday she would get everything ready for the hike, and Saturday morning she would leave. *Please don't let it come to that, God,* she prayed.

The fishing was fantastic, and by nightfall Julie had seven walleyes and one northern pike lying on shore. She cut the fish up as best she could without a fillet knife and spent the evening cooking it. They ate their fill and washed it down with the last of the Coke.

The air search tuned up nothing after going on night and day for two days. There had been no signal from the transponder, and they didn't spot any wreckage. Thursday they would expand the search to the west, but the consensus among the pilots was that Arnie would never have been that far off course and it was a waste of time. If nothing was found by Friday night, the search would be called off, at least by the Civil Air Patrol. Arnie's buddy Irv wouldn't give up until he found him.

Irv and Arnie were like brothers. Well, older and younger brothers. Irv had about fifteen years on Arnie and he'd watched Arnie grow up and be a hockey star, never missing one of his games. He wrote him letters when Arnie was in the service for four years. They were fishing and hunting buddies, and had been best friends for years.

Irv had a family but he rarely talked about them. Although he and his wife still lived together it seemed their marriage existed only for the sake of their kids. Irv provided for his family and was always there for his kids, but he never talked about his wife, and although that bothered Arnie, he didn't press him on it. It was one of those subjects that seemed to be off limits, and that was fine. Irv told Arnie more than once how lucky he was to have Julie, but on the other hand, he seemed to be jealous of their relationship and was not overly friendly towards her.

Irv was always at the airport when Arnie went there, and when Arnie became a pilot Irv was one of his instructors. In the years since then, they had flown all over the country together, and the talks they had in the aircraft showed how much they thought alike, despite the difference in their ages. Irv also understood what it was like to be down in a plane in this wilderness area. The odds weren't good, even if you survived the landing.

The word was passed to campers and canoers in the area that a plane was down and to report anything out the ordinary, like oil in the water or a burned area but it was late for the camping and hiking season so there wouldn't be a lot of people in the area.

By Thursday morning the weather had warmed up considerably. It was Indian summer in the wilderness area and it felt good. Julie sat in the sun with her shirt off and let the sun warm her sore chest. In a few minutes, she would have to try to swim across to the other side. It wasn't that far, but the water was very cold, and the sooner she got over there the better. Julie was a strong swimmer, but she would use one of the seat cushions out of the plane for a life preserver just in case. With her sore arm, she had no idea whether swimming was going to work or not.

She took Timmy back up into the plane to stay while she was gone, and talked to Arnie. It shouldn't take more than a couple of hours to get to the end of the lake, once she got to the far shore, and the same amount of time to return, so she should be back by supper. She had little luck getting clothes to dry lately, so she would take them off and put them in a Ziploc bag that had been in the suitcase, and then put them back on when she got to the opposite shore. The only other clothes she had packed were dress clothes, which were useless out here.

Julie kissed Arnie and Timmy good-bye, slid down the wing, and walked to the shore with Jake following. She undressed and put her clothes in the bag. She zipped it up tight and put it under her arm. It felt funny to be naked and standing on the shore, even though there wasn't a soul around. *Maybe if she stood here for a while, someone would come by just to see her hooters* she thought. *Heck, she would give them a lap dance for a ticket out of here.* The thought made her laugh out loud, but the smile left her face as she waded into the lake. It was cold. Damn cold. She waded out for quite a ways before the water got deep, and she began her swim to the other shore.

With the help of her clothing bag and seat cushion, she made it over in short time, Jake chugging along behind her. Julie ran out of the water and found a big rock that had been warmed by the sun. She sat on it shivering and warmed up while dripping dry, and Jake found another dead fish to eat. Dressed again, she walked the shoreline as best she could. There were a lot of rocks, and in some places the rocks were huge cliffs that went right to the water's edge, and she had to retreat inland. But the lake wasn't that big, and she saw the river before she ever got to it, so she turned around and went back. It was Kato Lake.

Arnie was excited to see her and glad that she had found the river. He would have rather been on Sand Point Lake, but at least now they knew. They sat in the plane and talked while Julie dried her hair with one of Arnie's shirts. She would pack one extra set of clothes for both her and Timmy in case they got wet, but that's all she could carry. She would also bring the fishing rod and some tackle. Arnie showed her how to roll everything up in the blanket and then roll it all up again in the tarp. He had her cinch it up with his belt, as he certainly didn't have any use for it and there were other concerns. The lighter was getting low on fluid, so she was going to have to use it sparingly. Fish and water would be their diet. Arnie's diet until they got back was going to consist of twenty-three bottles of home brew, and whatever fish Julie caught and cooked before she left.

Julie made one of the plane floats into a boat that she thought she could use to push Timmy to the other side. It had broken off on impact and was lying in the woods. He would straddle it like a horse to keep him out of the water, and they could tie their roll of clothes and blankets on top. She would have to brave it at least once more, the icy-cold trip to the opposite shore line.

Arnie drew the map for her and showed her how to follow it and look for landmarks. He estimated that it would be about eighty miles to the nearest road, but he hoped she would run into campers long before that. The only problem was that it was late enough in the year that there wouldn't be many campers around.

They would spend tonight in the plane as a family, for what they hoped would not be the last time, and poor Jake had to stay on the ground. They talked into the night and shared two bottles of home brew, which on their empty stomachs gave them a bit of a buzz and then Julie softly sang Timmy to sleep. Arnie cried when she sang. He loved her so much.

Arnie had regained a little more movement in his arms. He looked at the sore under Julie's arm and said it looked like it was healing, so he wasn't going to remove the clot over the hole. Arnie had been a medic in the army, so he had some experience with injuries, and it made Julie feel better to have him look at it. The 'road rash', as Arnie put it, on her breast was healing fine, and with a devilish grin he offered to rub ointment on it. Julie said she would pass on that, at least for now, but his light heartedness about their physical conditions did inspire her.

By Friday night most of the search had been called off. They would ask people flying in the area to keep their eyes peeled, but otherwise there was not a lot more they could do until they got a break or somebody found something. Searches cost a lot of money and took a lot of resources that they really didn't have right now. On the other hand Arnie was well known and a barrage of phone calls from Shirley Capes, Irv, and his readers came in, but to no avail. For now, the search was off.

Arnie's mother still sat in the porch and stared at the lake. She was a simple woman and felt so helpless and left out. She had no idea where to go with her concerns. Each day without some sign of them deepened her depression, but she tried to maintain hope with her constant prayers. She only left her chair for more cigarettes and coffee and Irv's visits seemed to give her some hope.

Julie's folks weren't very optimistic and spent a lot of time on the phone with Irv and the Duluth Air Base. Each day without any news was taking its toll on them. They loved their only daughter very much. They wanted and wished for so much more for her out of life when she first started going with Arnie. They didn't have anything against Arnie, but they felt that Timmy would be a hardship for her with his problems. They knew the problems that came with a special child like that, first hand. They longed for grandchildren of their own, but as time passed and they saw how attached Julie was to Arnie and Timmy, they both had relented and accepted Arnie and his family. Besides, Julie said that if she ever got a deal in writing from the guy, there would be more babies.

CHAPTER 7

▼

For the rest of Thursday Julie rested and made preparations. She seemed more self-confident now than she had been since the crash, despite the fact that there had been nothing good happening to encourage her. Maybe it was just that to had kicked in, and maybe she was just facing reality the best she could, but it was helping her make good decisions. She'd always been a strong person, but the crash, had just over whelmed her.

The fishing was still good, and she caught several more, and let Timmy help land them. He squealed with delight and it felt good to find something that made him happy. The fish would last them for a few days. She cooked them in the hard hat and then packaged them in the old cracker wrappers to keep them clean and as fresh as she could.

She was still very worried about Arnie. There was one thing she couldn't help Arnie with, and that was a bowel movement. She didn't dare move him, and doubted she could, even if his back wasn't broken. Julie wanted to approach the issue with him, but then thinking it would only depress him further, she didn't. The main thing right now was for her to find help before Arnie starved or died of dehydration.

She had everything packed on Friday, but they would wait one more day. They had yet to hear or see another aircraft and planes weren't supposed to fly over this area below five thousand feet, so unless someone was looking for them they weren't going to see one, either.

Arnie had given up on the transponder. It must not be working. He worked on his map and drew a line for Julie to follow. It would eventually bring her out onto a country road about fifty aeronautical miles south of them, and it would probably require about eighty miles of walking, some of it through rough terrain. She would have to cross the river at the end of Kato Lake right away. The river was only seven miles long and ran between Kato and Rainbow, the next lake south. If she tried to go around Kato the other way, she would walk through an almost impenetrable swamp that was shown on the map. He had worked on the map all day until darkness overtook him. but it gave him purpose. His physical condition would not allow for much helping, so now he had to work with his mind to try and help. He needed to be part of the solution.

Timmy would be Julie's biggest problem. How far could you expect an eight year old to walk in one day? This seemed to bother Arnie more than Julie.

"I think that I need to make it as much of a game as I can," she told Arnie. Timmy was easily entertained, but when not busy he seemed to get moody and unpredictable. So far he had been pretty good, but he too had a breaking point, and she didn't want to see that. Also, the medicine that controlled his behavior would last only a few more days. Because this medicine also made him less energetic, Arnie suggested they split the pills in half. It might be good if he were more energetic, as long as she could control him.

Arnie's injuries seemed to be serious but not life threatening. All of his bodily functions seemed to work fine. Julie had filled all of the empty pop and beer bottles with water and those and the beer he had left, with some fish, would keep him going for a while. The interior of the plane was still fairly watertight and would keep him dry and somewhat warm, unless it became unseasonably cold.

So now it was just some psychological questions that were left to both of their imaginations. How long could you sit in a plane seat looking at the top of a tree before you went out of your mind? But Arnie, too was a survivor, and he also believed that Julie would succeed. If he had to die he was right where he wanted to be: in a plane in the wilderness. He would have preferred a plane not leaning against a tree, but what the hell. You couldn't have everything.

He asked Julie to leave the notepad, as thoughts of what he would write if no one came were on his mind. If there was one thing Arnie did well, it was write. Irv had always said, *"Arnie could sell sand to an Arab if he could just write him a letter."* Arnie thought about Irv and knew that his friend was probably looking for him every day. Yesterday while napping he had awakened suddenly when he thought he heard Irv's voice calling from across the water. It had been almost eerie at the time, but it did give him hope.

Irv was still flying everyday He could not, and would not give up. He had covered the entire route several times, and now his trips were taking him closer and closer to where Arnie had crashed. He couldn't bring himself to believe that Arnie would be this far southwest, but he was running out of places to look. The one thought that did run through his mind was that Arnie had crashed into a lake and sunk, but he doubted it. Arnie had dead-sticked planes before, and was too good a pilot for that to happen.

On Friday night Julie brought Timmy up into the plane and they spent their last night all together. Julie washed Arnie once more before they went to sleep. She combed his beard and his hair, all the while crying softly, while Arnie stared at her through his own tear-rimmed eyes. She rested her head on his shoulder and slept fitfully through the night. She was not close to God in her everyday life, but she found herself forming prayers that he would help her get out and find help. There were just so many unknowns out there. She always had fears of animals in the forests, despite Arnie's insistence that they were more afraid of you then you were of them. No one could be more scared than she was right now, but she had to be brave for Arnie.

The next morning Arnie held her as well as he could and said, "Julie, I know you'll get us out of this but it won't be easy. Try to stay as dry as you can, and follow the map. Pick out a spot on the horizon and walk to it, and then do it again. It will keep you from walking in circles. It is important that you stay on course. If someone does find me, I'll know approximately where you should be on any given day. Jake should alert you to any animal trouble, but outside of wolves and bears, you should be all right. Just remember, they are probably more afraid of you than you are of them."

Julie smiled and said, "Any wolf that would be that scared would be slipping in a lot of shit, Arnie." Her half-hearted attempt at humor broke the seriousness of the conversation.

Arnie laughed and said, "I love you, darling," and kissed the ring she now wore. He then kissed her mouth one last time, and hugged Timmy for a long moment. "Be brave, buddy," he said.

They were wearing all of the clothes they could wear, but for the swim to the mainland it would be strip time again. She hadn't been naked in front of Timmy for a while, but if it bothered him at all he didn't say anything. Julie had taken off his pants, shoes, and socks and had him straddle the float. She stuffed everything else into the tarp and tied it to the strut still sticking up, which also was a good handle for Timmy to hang onto. Unlike the day of her last swim, it was chilly out, about-forty-five-degrees, so she wanted to get this over with as quickly as possible.

The wind was against them, so after shoving off, Julie waded as far as she could, and then grabbed the end of the float and kicked hard as she could to propel them. She was trying to keep from going into shock from the cold water. Timmy thought it was a great ride and laughed and tried to kick his legs, but Julie warned him to sit still so they didn't tip over. He had no life jacket and she had only one good arm.

Jake stood on shore for a while, not knowing if he was supposed to come or not. Julie heard his barking and saw him running up and down the shoreline, and eventually the big Labrador jumped in and swam alongside. He was a powerful swimmer and the cold water didn't bother him a bit. Her arms were getting stiff and she felt a cramp in her side at about the same time her feet touched bottom and they pushed up on the opposite shore. With the float pushed up on land where it could be seen from the air, she dressed quickly before she grew any colder than she already was. They needed to start walking to warm up, and fast. She dressed Timmy and, taking his hand, they looked one last time at the island and the white plane showing through the trees, and then started their journey. "I love you, Arnie," she shouted across the water, but there was no answer.

She had Arnie's cell phone, but the batteries were nearly dead so she kept it shut off. Maybe in a day or so she would check for a signal, but so far there had been nothing.

The walk was slow at first because Julie was holding Timmy's hand with Jake bringing up the rear. With the pack on her back and both of them hand in hand, it made slow going through the brush. They stopped to rest for a minute, and Julie sat down with Timmy and explained that he would have to walk right behind her. Timmy nodded his head as if he understood. His vocabulary was only a few words, but with a little encouragement he could understand a lot. Julie felt so bad for him. There was already scratches on his face from the brush and a few surviving mosquitoes had found him too.

They walked for nearly two hours before they found themselves at the river. They sat on the bank and Julie made them a little lunch with fish and a few crackers she had saved for Timmy. Poor Jake looked so pitifully hungry, but Julie didn't know what to do for him. She finally gave him a little fish, and she caught a couple of frogs, which he ate. They walked up the river to find a shallow spot to cross, and Julie found a wild rice patch. She took off her jeans and waded out and collected all she could reach in the tin hard hat that was her cooking kettle. She had cooked rice lots of times, and this was going to be a special treat. She soon had the hat full and waded back in to shore, chilled to the bone. She had had Timmy down for while and cautioned him to stay there while she was collecting rice. He wasn't sleeping, but just watching her, sucking on his fingers and although. it bothered her that he was so troubled, she was also encouraged, for things had gone well so far with him leaving Arnie. Then the thought that they had gone two miles out of a possible eighty put it back in perspective. "*I need to not play mind games with myself so much. These roller coaster emotions are going to be dangerous.*"

She could still see the lake but as soon as they crossed the river it would be behind them and so would Arnie. For a moment she realized that as long as she could see the lake she knew where Arnie was but that was soon going to change. Once again she felt like crying and just picking Timmy back up and going back, telling Arnie she couldn't do it. She sat down next to Timmy and held his head in her lap. Then the words came to her as if Arnie had shouted them from the plane: "*Time to grow up, Julie, and get walking.*"

The river didn't look too deep, but there was no way of knowing until they started crossing, and this was the narrowest spot they had found. She stripped Timmy down and they started out hand in hand. It was rocky on the river bottom so Julie left their shoes on. They didn't want any cut feet. The water did get up to Julie's chest, so she had to hold Timmy up with her sore arm and hold all of their possessions above water with the other arm, but it was a short trip and they were soon on the other side. She dressed them both quickly and they started walking down the riverbank, squishing in their shoes, but happy that they could probably leave their clothing on for the rest of the trip. *I've had my clothes on and off more in the last two days than some of the strippers in downtown Duluth,* she thought to herself.

It was seven miles to Rainbow Lake, the next stop on their map. One of the things Arnie had been hopeful for was that they would meet some late-season campers. This wasn't an established route for canoers, but sometimes people who were looking for something off the beaten path would venture onto these lakes.

For Irv Engstrom it was day six in a fruitless search. On Wednesday he had called the Civil Air Patrol to express his frustration with them for quitting the air search so soon, but he didn't change anybody's mind and it ended with him shouting and hanging the phone up in anger. Today he would be searching an area just five miles east of the island where Arnie was. After going over weather records of the day of the flight, Irv had thought that just maybe Arnie might have gone west to avoid that storm. But how far west and how much area could one-man cover, by himself? The search was taking a toll on Irv, both emotionally and financially. Irv pretty much lived from payday to payday, and the gasoline cost alone for his aircraft had reached into the hundreds of dollars.

There was also the problem of flying low enough to see the terrain and not running into anything. It was not exactly flat down there, and early morning fog was prevalent on many occasions, especially over water, which was exactly where he needed to search.

There had been a message for him to call Shirley Capes at a Duluth newspaper when he got home on Saturday. At first he wasn't going to call. *It's just another damn reporter,* he said to himself. Then he relented and called. The phone rang several times before someone with a sleepy voice picked up the receiver.

"This is Irv Engstrom," he said. "You left a message for me to call you."

"Irv," The call had surprised her and she took a second to think what she was going to say. "Thank you for calling, Irv. This is Shirley Capes from the newspaper in Duluth where Arnie Bottelmiller worked,—works." Shirley had been napping and she stopped to clear her throat and light up a smoke. "Sorry about that," she said resuming her conversation. "Irv, I saw you on the news the other day and you said you were a close friend of Arnie's, and I just wondered if anything is still being done to look for his plane? I know the organized search was called off."

"I'm doing as much as one man can," Irv said back sarcastically. "Why does it concern you? You reporters could do a lot more good talking to the Civil Air Patrol and encouraging them to keep looking for Arnie instead of bothering me."

"No, look. Please listen to me." Shirley said somewhat exasperated. "I'm not a reporter. I'm calling as Arnie's friend. I need to know what I can do to help you."

Irv ran his hands through his gray wavy hair and sat down at his kitchen table. "I guess the one thing I am going to need is either more people to help with more planes, or some help with the expense of all this. I don't have much money, and it has taken all I have to keep my plane in the air. I have a family I haven't seen in over a week."

"Irv," Shirley said. "I can help you financially. Send me the name of your bank and I'll have money wired to you. If you have friends that will help the search, I'll pay for them too."

"Gee … thanks," Irv said, taken by surprise. "I guess I don't know what to say. Look I'm sorry if I was short with you. It's just that has been—."

"Irv," Shirley cut him off. "Arnie is a great friend of mine, too. I want to help any way I can. Look, I'll call you tomorrow. What time is good?"

"Evening," Irv said.

"I will get back to you, I promise she said," and then hung up.

Shirley stood at the large picture window of her house high on a hillside over-looking the Duluth skyline. It was dark in the room and the red glow of her ciga-rette butt was all that gave evidence that somebody was there. Arnie had to be down there somewhere alive. She just knew it, or was it false hope? She never got to know Julie or Timmy, so it was hard for her to identify with their plight, although she did think of them.

Why couldn't I have left well enough alone she thought? If I hadn't got involved Arnie would still be here writing for all of us. She bit her lip and stubbed out her cigarette. She hadn't cried since Edgar died, and then not for long. There hadn't been time for it … she had a newspaper to care for. What she wouldn't give now to have someone to share her fears and grief with, just someone to hold her and talk to her. She had very few friends and, Arnie had been as close as she had gotten to anyone she worked with. It was lonely at the top. She poured her-self a brandy and swirled it around in the snifter before downing the warm liquid in one gulp. Shirley wiped her mouth with the back of her hand and sat back on the couch, still looking out the window. The tears were coming now and it was sweet relief almost as if something had been unlocked inside of her. She reached for the bottle again and held it to her breast while she uncapped it. She could see far out over the city buildings with all of their lights, into the harbor, and beyond. This was the city she had grown up in and worked in all of her life. She had married young, and was always too busy to have a family. Of course Edger never wanted kids. He was married to his job and then the accident happened and she was all alone. *You never thought about that, Edger, did you? You just figured we would both fade away together someday.* This time she ignored the glass and drank right from the bottle.

Many miles out, a lonely freighter headed for an eastern port, its green and red running lights growing dimmer by the minute. It seemed so all-alone in that vast sea and that's how Shirley thought Arnie must feel if he is down in that wilder-ness.

She tipped the bottle and splashed some more into her glass. *Well she did have one friend tonight didn't she?* She kissed the bottle and held it between her legs.

If Irv had been a few hundred feet higher, when he flew over that next morn-ing, he might have seen the float Julie had left on the beach. He passed two miles to the east of the island, but the tree line prevented him from seeing the beach itself, and when he returned, the trees on the island hid it.

Arnie heard the aircraft, but there was little he could do but wait and pray he would be spotted. The roar of the engines told him that the plane was almost overhead, but he could see nothing, and then the engine noise faded away, never to return. From the air, the wreck was almost impossible to see, as the spreading branches of the one-hundred-year-old tree were like a canopy over the plane. Part of one wing that was too heavy for Julie to carry was the only thing sticking out from under the trees' protection and it was in heavy brush.

Arnie had never been a religious man, at least not in the sense that he attended a regular church service. He did believe in God, but felt the best way he could worship God was to be a good person and do all he could to preserve this wonderful wilderness he lived next to. His mother had brought him up in the Lutheran church, but neither he nor Julie had gone for years, except for weddings and funerals. This beautiful land was his religion.

Arnie had prayed a lot during the last few days. Right now God was the only one he had to talk to, and right now he needed help like he had never needed it before. He promised God that when he got out of this mess, he would be a better person and he asked him to be with Julie, and give her strength, and to calm Timmy's troubled mind so he wouldn't be a hindrance to Julie.

He had a beer in the afternoon, and that relaxed him somewhat. He would have to ration them out and be careful he didn't drink more than he should and get tipsy. Arnie's home brew had quite a kick, and on an empty stomach it didn't take much. He was using the empties to pee into because he had lost his cardboard tube. When they were full he tossed them out the window.

He was so disappointed about that plane not returning earlier that he almost said the hell with it and drank a second one, but he caught himself just before the plane returned. This time it was farther away and on his right instead of the left. It was west of him and Arnie knew it was a search plane. No one else would have permission to fly that low except the Forest Service.

He wondered about Julie's progress. Why couldn't it have been him who was walking out? She was hiding her pain. He was sure of that. He had tried not to scare her but her shoulder injury looked pretty bad. Was she capable of doing what she had to do?

Arnie broke down and cried softly, until he went to sleep.

It was getting dark and Irv was going home. He had no plans to come back to this area. He was going to go back to the original flight plan and cover that area again. There was no way Arnie would have been this far off course but first he needed to rest and get his head screwed on right and pay some attention to his own family. He would make some phone calls tonight and see if he could get some help. That is if he got the money.

CHAPTER 8

▼

His name was Eetah, which in wolf language meant "stealthy one." Canis Lupus was his technical name. He had been born two years ago this spring, to part of a litter of five. His parents were the alpha leaders of the pack, which consisted of eight adult wolves and two litters of pups. Eetah was one of five pups, three females and two males, but one of his sisters had died and his mother had sadly taken the body away. All the other adult wolves in the pack were his uncles and aunts. The whole pack was his family and they were all excited about the pups.

He was born in early April, blind and deaf as all wolf pups are, and weighing barely a pound. Eetah and his siblings were all black at birth, but as they got older they turned more of a gray color with some white mixed in. Their eyes were dark blue with round pupils.

For the first two weeks they could only crawl around the den, as their front legs had enough strength to propel, but their hind legs were not developed to that point yet. Gradually they learned to stand and chew on their mother's tail and legs when they weren't nursing. Their father and some of the rest of the pack either brought food for their mother or watched them while she hunted. She was a good mother and very protective of her cubs.

Eetah's mother dug the den on a sun-splashed hillside next to a bubbling creek. It was nearly fifteen feet deep before it widened into a room that was almost four square feet. There was a low spot in the tunnel to catch water so it couldn't get into the den. She kept the den clean and orderly, the same as she did with her pups.

One day when they were about three weeks old, the weather warmed enough for them to go outside and play in the sun. Mother was always close by, and once when an eagle had flown low overhead, she rushed them back into the den. It was their first lesson in survival and there were many more to come. They established a pecking order amongst themselves and he had been recognized as the top pup. He was his mother's favorite, always the first one out of the den, and the most obedient of all of the pups.

At about six weeks of age they were weaned, and their mother and some of the rest of the pack would bring them regurgitated food to eat. They made regular trips to the nearby creek to drink and they played with each other every day, quickly gaining weight and strength.

Around July of that year, they were big enough to go with the pack and learn the hunting skills they would need to survive in the wilderness. Eetah weighed almost forty pounds by that time, and the other pups were not far behind. By the time winter came they would need to be able to hunt and do their share of help-ing to feed the pack.

His relationship with his father remained strained. Maybe it was because his father felt threatened by the growing pup. He knew that someday he would be challenged by this fast growing pup for the position of the leader of the pack.

His father was a stern leader and did not permit any foolishness or laziness among the other wolves in the pack. He was a majestic wolf that always walked with his head held high, his nose constantly testing the air for intruders. He was more than three feet long, not including his tail, and weighed almost ninety pounds. There were challenges by other adult wolves for his position, but he rebuffed them all easily.

Eetah progressed quickly as a hunter, and by the time his second birthday rolled around he was contributing more to the pack than almost any other wolf except his father. He once single-handedly brought down a large buck whitetail deer, which the pack had eaten on for a week. The buck had made a cut in Eetah's side with his antlers, and although it healed fine, he learned a valuable les-son about deer antlers. He would team up with his brother, and they would chase whitetails, often one of them waiting in seclusion while the other chased the deer to his brother. Eetah could run for miles, but when it came to stalking prey he could also be as quiet as a large cat gliding through the woods.

His second winter had been a hard one in the woods. It was severely cold and the snow depth reached three feet in many places. For the most part, the deep snow had helped them when chasing deer because deer couldn't run it in with their sharp hooves, and the wolves with their large feet were able to run on top of the packed snow. Many days it was just too cold to hunt, and they would hole up in their shelters. He hadn't been back to the den where he was born for some time. Eetah was running with a mate he had taken from a different pack, and his father had not tolerated her in his pack. Torn between his love for his family and his love for his new mate, he spent a lot of time with both of them, until his father solved the problem for him by banishing him from the pack in a short but bloodless fight.

It was spring again, and Eetah was two years old and fully-grown. He was bigger than his father, measuring almost three and one-half feet long and weighing 110 pounds. He had been forced to find new territory, and by July he still was looking for his own place.

It was also at this time that Eetah made a mistake that nearly cost him his life. Along with his mate, he tried to take a moose calf for a Sunday dinner when the bull moose intervened. Eetah, running from the big bull, slipped and fell from a rocky bluff into the lake some forty feet below. He hit a rock in the water, which broke his right leg, and although he made it to shore, he was practically immobile. His mate cared for him for a while, and then one day while she was hunting, a Forest Service worker who canoed into the area doing a wolf study discovered him. She called for help, and he was anesthetized with a tranquilizer gun and flown to a wolf center. His leg was put in a cast and he was allowed to recuperate.

It was this same contact with people that gave him some trust in them. He was never meant to be tamed, and every attempt had been made to avoid it. Six weeks later he was released back into the wild, at the same place where he was found. Within a few days he was back in business hunting, although limping slightly, but try as he might, he never saw his mate again.

Eetah watched Julie cross the river with Timmy and the yellow dog. Julie reminded Eetah of the woman who had helped him when he was hurt, but her scent was different. He didn't know what to make of the boy, and he was even more skeptical of the dog. The big wolf knew the dog possessed some of the same characteristics as he did, so he stayed his distance. He didn't fear the humans, but he did fear the dog, even though he was superior in strength and knew it.

Right now he didn't see the woman and the boy as prey, but the dog looked like a meal if he got hard up. It would be best to separate them somehow, but he wasn't giving too much thought about it at the moment. They walked along the riverbank, heading south into the territory he was trying to claim. They looked tired and confused, and the boy child was making a lot of crying noises. The woman would stop from time to time to comfort him. She was holding her arm funny, and Eetah sensed she was hurt. In fact, he could smell the sour stench of her injury, and it brought back memories of his own injury. The dog stayed close to them, just kind of loping along behind, and Eetah stayed back just enough to avoid the dog smelling him.

Julie wanted to get to Rainbow Lake before dark if she could. The weather was cooperating with high clouds that gave them some filtered sun. The terrain was rough, and it was not only brushy but it was also swampy, and several times they had to leave the riverbanks to detour around these areas. They weren't able to avoid all of them, so they had gotten quite wet and muddy. Julie also witnessed the return of her diarrhea and she was racked with cramps. She had to stop from time to time to try and relieve herself, but there was very little left in her. By four-thirty, just when it was getting to be dusk, they broke out onto the shores of Rainbow Lake.

It took a while for Julie to make a shelter for the night, but she found a large fir tree that had blown down and was lying on its side. It looked to have been dead for some time. She draped the tarp over the tree, and held the corners down with rocks. Breaking off most of the branches that were in the way, she used them to get a campfire going. Arnie's disposable lighter didn't have a lot of fluid left in it, but she was lucky it had been dry out, and she got a fire going quickly. She changed Timmy into some dry pants and underwear and also changed her pants. She only had one pair of jeans, but the cotton slacks she had brought along to sleep in would be fine until her jeans dried.

Julie cooked up some of the rice and the last of the fish in the old hard hat. The hat had been a shiny aluminum at one time, but it was now burnt black on the outside. They ate in silence, and this time Jake got a fish. Julie was confident she could catch some more after supper.

Timmy was exhausted so Julie lay down with him, singing softly to him, brushing his long brown hair with her fingertips until he went to sleep, and then picked out the brambles and burrs that were stuck in his hair. She loved Timmy so much and felt so bad that he had to make a trip like this. Maybe it was good that he didn't understand much of what was going on. He didn't have much of a sense of fear, never did have.

Her thoughts went back to Arnie, and she wondered how he was coping with his injuries and isolation. The thought came to her that she never really thought about what it would be like to be married to a paralyzed man. She shook the thoughts off, not wanting to deal with that now. She was getting ahead of the game. The more details she struggled with, the more depressed she was likely to get.

When Timmy was asleep, Julie left Jake to watch him. After putting the fishing rod together, she went down to the lake. It hurt to cast with her right arm and she wasn't very good at it with her left arm, but she did catch some bass by a log that was half floating in the lake. She just jiggled the bait off the edge of it, and before long she had a few fish, throwing them up on shore so they couldn't jump back in the lake. Just as she went to throw the last one, she slipped on the wet log and fell head first into the lake. The shock of the cold water was bad enough, but the fact that she dropped the rod and reel was worse. She made her way to shore and then turning around walked back out on the log. She could see the rod and reel on the bottom, so once more she braced herself and dove in after it.

Now both pairs of pants were wet. She put the still damp jeans back on, along with dry underpants and socks, and sat by the fire to dry out. She thought about Arnie again and started to cry. *It's hard damn it. It was so damn hard. Why God, does all of this have to happen to me?* She was so lonely and scared. There were times in their relationship that she was not as strong as she wanted to be, but Arnie had been always there to encourage her and make it all right. She had prided herself in being strong but she was now realizing that so much of that strength had come from Arnie. *Now she had no choice but to be the strong one and she was just no damn good at it.* She curled up next to Jake for warmth and went to sleep. "Help me Jake," she said out loud. Jake was not sleeping very soundly.

Jake smelled the wolf as he had tried to get closer to them, and he now sat up growling, his hackles rising high on his back. Eetah also heard Jake and retreated back to a safe area. Julie tried to see into the darkness, but there didn't appear to be anything out there. She listened carefully, and all she could hear was the water lapping on the shore. The fire that had died down almost to nothing now came back to life as she got up and added more wood to it. Jake, still disturbed, lay back down, satisfied that whatever was out there had left, but he knew it could return.

Eetah meant them no harm; he only wanted to find out more about them. He smelled Jake's scent glands when he was aroused, and that turned him around more than anything. He was hungry, come to think of it, so he wandered off to hunt.

Arnie wasn't having an easy time. The plane flying over the other day had left him more depressed than before, and he was also worried about Julie and Timmy, but he had little control over that anymore. Arnie spent the whole morning thinking about his injuries and what kind of a life he would have if he was rescued. Was life going to be worth living? Reality told him he would never fly again or make love to Julie or run with Timmy. Would Julie leave him? Wasn't it bad enough she was caring for his child and now she would have to be a nurse to him too? Maybe it would be best if he did die. Then he wouldn't be burden to anyone and they would remember him as he once was, not as a hopeless cripple. On the other hand he was regaining a little more movement in his left arm and now could bring his hand up to his mouth. He would die for a bag of Beechnut chew right now.

Irv had given up the search for now. He called Shirley and thanked her for her support, but right now, unless they got a lead, he was out of places to look and was needed at home and at work. There was a time when he thought the people in the Civil Air Patrol were a bunch of quitters, but now he was facing up to the same reality that finally had made them stop looking.

He drove out to the house and visited with Arnie's mom, who insisted that she wanted to stay at her son's house for the time being. She still had hope, and Irv still had hope too, but he needed something concrete to go on.

CHAPTER 9

▼

Julie woke to the soft patter of rain on the canvas. Her back was soaking wet, as they were sleeping in a depression in the ground. Timmy was awake and looking at her quizzically. Jake was the only one still sleeping, although Julie thought he was faking and gave him a playful kick to get him off of her feet. When she stuck her head outside, the sky didn't look like it was going to clear anytime soon. It was raining and gray clouds stretched from horizon to horizon.

She had a few fish from last night and enough rice for a couple of meals, but she wasn't going to get a fire started in this weather. It was cold and miserable, and for a few minutes the tears came again. She turned her head so Timmy wouldn't see them. That wasn't going to solve anything though, and Julie quickly composed herself, wiping her nose on her sleeve and her tears on top of Timmy's head. At times like this it was good to be like Timmy, who had no realization of the trouble they were in. In fact, his life was lived hour to hour. Maybe she could practice being like that for a while and it might keep her from dwelling on the days to come. She patted the back of her head and felt her hair all snarled together. *I should do something with this rat's nest,* she thought and then laughed out loud. "Oh, I'm losing it." she said.

If they walked in the rain they were going to get soaked, more so than they already were. The last thing she needed was for her or Timmy to get sick. She knew they needed to get out of these woods as soon as possible, but she made the decision to stay put for now.

She cleaned the fish that she had caught yesterday, and then made a small fire under the shelter of their canvas. By raising the canvas as high as she could on one side of the shelter, and with the wind behind them, she was able to direct most of the smoke away and still keep the fire out of the rain. The tree they were under was a virtual bonanza of firewood. A short time later she cooked the fish, made a little more rice, and they ate. The fire helped to dry out some of their wet clothes and give them a little bit of warmth. Julie studied the map Arnie had drawn and came to the conclusion that the next ten miles or so were going to be the worst. Up to this point they had followed either a river or a lakeshore, but now they were going to be forced to leave the lake and head due south, through the woods to the Sawbuck River. Once she found the river, she would follow it to Heron Lake, and then continue following it to the far end of the lake. She didn't want to look any further ahead than that right now.

Julie was amazed at how well Timmy had fared so far. She thought he would be bored and become unmanageable. Goodness knows he could get that way at home even on a good day. The medicine helped, but he had to be uncomfortable and bored silly. Right now he was digging a hole with a stick, and Jake was helping him. Poor Jake. His ribs were showing and he wasn't as energetic as he usually was. Maybe when they got going again, they would find something for him to eat.

About noon the rain quit. Julie waited a few minutes to make sure it had stopped, then bundled things up and they set off. Her diarrhea seemed to be under control and she felt better today than she had since the accident. The diarrhea had to be from the infection under her arm, and not from what they were eating, because so far Timmy was fine, and he was eating what she was eating. There wasn't much food left and that was a problem. She no longer had an open sore under her arm, but she did have a lump about the size of a golf ball there. It was sensitive and restricted her arm movement. The rest of her bruises had pretty well healed.

The walking was easier when they got away from the lake because the brush thinned out and the woods were more mature. The ground was more solid and they were making better time. *If only I knew where the hell south was,* Julie thought to herself.

She knew that moss grew on the north side of the trees and Arnie had told her to pick out a spot on the horizon and walk toward it. "*Easy for you to say, Arnie,*" she mused. It was impossible to see over the trees. She kept the wind in her face but she knew it could change, so she didn't want to rely on that too much.

Eetah had left for a while last night to hunt. The rain didn't bother him any, but it kept most of the animals in their holes or dens, so the hunting wasn't the best. He had followed two deer for a while, but they caught wind of him and scampered away. Then, just before dawn a cottontail rabbit hadn't been so lucky and ended up in his jaws. It was a good-sized rabbit and made a perfect meal. He slept for a few hours after he ate and then made his way back to Julie.

He smelled the fire and watched them for a while from about a hundred yards away, and then tiring of that, he went exploring. He hadn't seen any other wolves in the woods but he smelled their scent patches and knew that he wasn't alone. He saw a black bear that morning and watched her tear apart a beehive and eat the honey. When she left, he enjoyed the leftovers, but the bees bothered him so he didn't stay very long. He didn't consider bears his enemies, as they avoided him, but he didn't want one for a friend either. One of the wolves in his father's pack had been badly mauled by a mother bear when he attempted to kill a bear cub. The cub had gone up a tree, but mama was watching and had nailed him good.

Wolves love family structure, and Eetah had no one and was lonely. He wanted to find a mate before winter to correct that. Eetah missed his old friend and was convinced that maybe someday he would find her again, although any receptive female would be fine right now. It was either that or find a pack and challenge the leader to become the alpha wolf, but that was a rough way to get accepted. So far, the wolves he had met shied away from him. Maybe it was the collar that was left around his neck after his broken leg was fixed. Eetah had tried to get it off many times, but had finally given up. Although it didn't seem to hurt anything, he still didn't like it. The people at the wolf center were keeping tabs on him by tracking him through that transmitter, but they hadn't tried to find him for quite a while. He was doing fine as far as they were concerned, but they would look for him once more before the batteries gave out.

Arnie amused himself with a squirrel that had taken up residence in the plane with him. It spent the day scurrying back and forth bringing acorns into the cockpit and putting them in the hole in Julie's seat where the branch had ripped it open. Whenever Arnie moved, it would sit on the dash and chatter at him, somehow realizing that Arnie wasn't a threat to him. Not right now anyway. It also was crippled and held one back leg up when it scampered around, but had adapted and was remarkably agile. It gave Arnie some hope for himself.

He used his time to write down some notes to use for future newspaper articles if he got out of here alive. It was hard to keep his train of thought however, as he was always interrupted with some kind of panic attack. He turned his thoughts to Julie, who to him was so perfect, and although he felt that he didn't deserve her they would be so good together, if only they could survive this predicament they were in. *I will make all of this up to her by being more compromising and doing things she likes to do too* he thought. *Too much has been about me.* He always wanted to write a novel and felt that he could be successful doing that.

His stomach was not a problem. He had been terribly hungry for a few days, but then the hunger pains went away and a couple bottles of brew a day now seemed sufficient. He didn't want to think about what he would do when the beer ran out. The boredom was bad, but the pencil and paper helped somewhat. On the last page of the tablet, he started a last letter to Julie. But that was too depressing right now, and he still had too much hope yet to complete it. It was something that he wanted to write before he went out of his mind.

Arnie worried about Julie and Timmy constantly and prayed that God would guide them safely out. In fact, Arnie was praying more now than he ever had before, and it did bring him comfort. He used to have a little Bible that he read from time to time, when he was in the service, and Oh how he wished he had it now. How he wished he had anything to read.

On what ever day this was Irv made another trip to Duluth to plead for another search, but in the meantime another plane had gone down in Lake Superior, and that was their immediate concern. It was not a good day to talk with them. They did tell him to come back in a day or two, and they would discuss it then. It would soon be a week since Arnie and his family had taken off, so most people were now thinking of a body recovery, not a rescue mission.

Arnie's mother remained steadfast in her faith that her son would survive, and she stayed on the porch, watching the lake for him to return. She was a simple woman who believed in Gods will. Life hadn't been easy for her but she had learned to roll with the punches.

Julie's parents on the other hand were devastated and went into seclusion. They didn't have much hope that Julie, Timmy and Arnie had survived. In fact Julie's father was overly pessimistic about their likely demise and brought Julie's mother's spirits down along with his. He chased all the reporters off his property, cursing at them, and the media instead of ignoring them, and accusing them of being insensitive. The only information they were getting now was from the papers and from Irv who called them every day.

Julie, Timmy and Jake walked later that day than she had planned to, but she wanted to make up for some of the time they had lost waiting for the rain to stop that morning. The woods were now changing from aspen and birch to more of the hardwoods like oak and maple, and the ground was covered with leaves so it was easy walking. There were also a lot of mature white pines like the one Arnie had used for target practice with his plane. They were also heading gradually uphill. It started with a few small inclines, and now it was more like rock ridges. Upon reaching the top of the last ridge they were going to climb that day, Julie looked behind her and could see Rainbow Lake in the distance. When she looked on the map, it didn't look like they had covered much ground, but it did look like they were headed in the right direction. For the first time in a while, she was upbeat. Maybe this would work out, after all. *If only Arnie was holding out all right.*

Around five, Timmy refused to walk anymore, so Julie relented and set up camp. It was getting dark anyway. She searched for another tree to drape the tarp over and found one partway down the ridge. She cleared some branches from the tree, made a shelter, and then built a fire. It was going to be just a few mouthfuls of fish tonight; she wanted to save the rest of the rice for morning.

It might be easier walking away from the lakes and rivers, but it was also going to be easier to get lost, and up until now all of their food had come from the water. This was a big thing because the fish and rice were almost gone and Julie had no idea where they were going to get more. She filled several plastic pop bottles she had brought along with rainwater, hoping that it would last for a few days.

Jake had been gone for about a half an hour and although Julie whistled for him a few times, she hadn't seen him, and was beginning to worry. He smelled dead flesh and found what was left of a deer kill. He was so famished, he ate his fill, even though he could hear Julie whistling. Eventually he left the deer, choosing not to ignore her any longer.

The deer kill wasn't Eetah's but that of another wolf. Eetah laid high on the ridge and watched the dog eat. If he wanted to confront Jake, this would be the perfect time, but he was still full of rabbit meat and still a bit wary of the yellow Lab. There had been dogs at the wolf center, but he never confronted one face to face.

"Jake, where were you?" Julie scolded him. Jake just sat with his head hung and looked at the ground. Julie could smell the rotten meat on his breath and she knew what had happened. She couldn't blame him, so she kept quiet and picked the brambles from his fur.

It was a great night if you loved camping. The wind had died down to nothing, and the stars were brighter than she ever remembered seeing them. Julie spooned herself around Timmy and sang softly to him until he went to sleep, while Jake lay on the other side, still wondering what he had gotten scolded for.

When Timmy was asleep, Julie got up and walked over to the fire and sat down next to it. She hugged her legs and rested her head on her knees as she watched the glint of the fire reflecting off the ring Arnie had bought her. For many people an engagement was the first step to a long and happy marriage and was a very happy occasion. Something you shared with all your friends and relatives. For Julie, at least for now, that sharing was with her future stepson and a yellow Labrador dog. She giggled at the thought. Maybe if she found some food they could have a party. Do you suppose anyone had dropped a cake mix out here, and an oven, and a cake pan? Hell, let's wish for some hamburger too. My God she was going goofy she thought. But it helped to lighten her mood.

She dozed off and was awakened by Jake barking at something, and she hushed him so she could find out what had disturbed him. Out of the corner of her eye she saw the wolf standing on the ridge, silhouetted in the bright moonlight. It stood motionless and the moon was shown on it like a theater spotlight. It was Eetah.

He was a nocturnal creature by nature, and these people were making him tired with their sleeping habits. He walked back down the ridge a short way and curled up and went to sleep with his ears cocked, guessing he would have to change his habits a little. Far away and below him, a chorus of howling wolves sent a warning through the still night that this was their territory, and they would do whatever they could to retain it. They too had smelled the humans, but they had also smelled Eetah and they were more upset about him than they were about the human intruders.

Maybe it was her stomach growling that awoke her, or was it Jake? She laid thinking for a few minutes, was this day three or four? It had to be three but she didn't care anymore. She stirred the fire and poured water in the helmet for the last of the rice and fish. If they didn't find some food on their travels today, they were going to be shit out of luck. *I'm in a pissy mood today* she thought. *Maybe I'm getting my period. That's all I need.* She put aside a small portion of rice for Timmy's supper. Jake eating that rotting deer helped, so she no longer felt sorry for him. He threw part of it up but he didn't waste it, he just had another hot meal. He would keep eating it until it stayed down. "You're gross Jake," she said to him.

She made sure the fire was out before they broke camp. They would walk the top of the ridge for a while, as it was going in the right direction and was easy walking. They were a motley-looking group if there ever was one. Julie's jeans had a few rips in them and her knees were showing. Her hair was matted to her face, and one of her tennis shoes had ripped down the side. She wore the burnt black … fire-blackened hard hat on her head right now because she it was easier than carrying it. From time to time it would fall down over her face and she would have to push it back up. Timmy's hair was greasy, and his hands and face were muddy from playing in the dirt but he didn't seem to mind. He carried the rod and reel case that held their fishing gear with the map rolled up inside. He would fall behind constantly, and Julie would have to keep prodding at him to keep him going. So far she had promised him a trip to Disneyland and a new dirt bike when they got home, and she was hoping his memory was as bad as she thought it was. She couldn't let him walk in front because he had no idea where they were going. In fact he had no idea *why* they were going. Jake just plodded along as he brought up the rear. He made some short side trips, but the scent of the wolves made him stay a little closer.

About noon they ran out of ridge and had to descend down to a low forest that was, once again, full of aspen and birch trees and lots of brush. Julie saw several deer, but mostly it was just the white flag of their tails as they sped off. Jake would get excited for a few minutes, but he was in no mood to chase them. He did have a little hunting success on the way when he came across a partridge that couldn't fly, and tried to run from them through the woods. He chased it down, and being the good retriever he was, brought it back to Julie, wagging his big tail, so proud of his feat. She praised the big dog lavishly and snapped the neck on the bird, which was still alive. They stopped to rest while she cleaned it with Arnie's pocketknife after pulling the feathers out. They would have supper tonight anyway.

They crossed the lowland and then a ridge, and then another lowland before they came to a particularly high rock ridge that resembled the one where they had spent the night before. They walked the top of it for a while, and then, off in the distance Julie saw what she thought was a lake. But they weren't supposed to find any more lakes. She stopped and took out the map and she checked it once more. There were no lakes on the map. *Your map is full of shit, Arnie,* she said to herself just before she spotted the tree they had slept under the night before.'

Julie started sobbing and Timmy was crying with her, although he didn't know why. *What a waste* she thought, *they had walked all day for nothing. They walked in a big ass circle, accomplishing nothing.* She looked at both of them. They were full of scratches and covered with mud. They were both tired and worn out, and now she was beyond sad. She was alternately crying and thinking what good does this do, and then saying out loud, "Damn it! I'll cry if I want to. It's my life and I didn't ask for any of this to happen." She went through the whole litany of emotions she had been through before. She cursed Arnie and his plane. She cursed his idea that she and his handicapped son could ever think of walking out of this wild god-forsaken place. At last, exhausted, she sat and held Timmy and quieted him down because he was crying now too.

"Mommy's so sorry Timmy, for getting upset. Getting us all upset. She needs to rest and so do you."

Jake sensing something needed fixing stretched up with his neck and head, and licked her face. Julie patted his head and rubbed his ears. She needed to get rational again. She put the tarp over the same tree, built a fire, and roasted their partridge.

CHAPTER 10

▼

Their bellies full, and exhausted from their useless trip during the day, they were fast asleep before eight o'clock. The night was uneventful, and they slept as well as you could on branches and leaves. The next morning Julie got up early to think about where she was going and to study her map. The map didn't show a lot of detail beyond the lakes and rivers. It showed land, but it was anyone's guess if it was swamp or a mountain.

She thought a couple of times about building a huge fire. Maybe that would get someone's attention. The place to build that would probably have been on the island with the plane, but that was hindsight. Arnie had told her a horror story about a couple of hunters in Canada, who had gotten lost and started a forest fire to bring help, but the wind had shifted and they died in their own fire. Not to mention the millions of dollars in damage. There were always campers building campfires in hundreds of places, so small fires didn't attract any attention and big ones were a dangerous move.

She walked up to the top of the ridge and looked at where she thought they had walked the day before. She couldn't see over the next ridge, but that was the location of the woods that they had gotten turned around in. She was going to have to be more careful this time and see if she could get it right. If they walked hard and got moving right away, there was a chance they could make it to the river in one day, but just a chance. They had to get there soon because they were out of food again. She had enough rice for Timmy for one meal and that was it.

During the night it rained on the island where Arnie was ... absolutely poured, dropping at least four inches, although it was dry where Julie and Timmy were. The wind had also blown hard, and at some point during the night the air-plane had slid down the tree trunk about five feet. Apparently the ground where the tail was buried became soggy enough, and the wind blowing into the belly of the plane gave it enough push to move it. Arnie didn't realize what was happening at first, and by the time he finally did, it was over.

This was a welcome relief. Now he was sitting at just a slight angle, instead of the forty-five degree angle the plane had settled into after the crash. When he opened the door now, it was just a couple of feet to the ground, and he could see the lake through the trees. This served to cheer him up a bit. He was still stuck there, and nobody knew where he was, but at least the scenery had changed a little and he was far more comfortable.

There was one more problem that Arnie had and could not deal with, and it had to do with personal hygiene. He stunk terribly and could only guess what was happening to his bottom. He had no feeling there, so if it hurt he wasn't aware of it, but he still wanted to take care of it if he could. Last night while it had rained, he had opened the door and let the water soak his lower half to see if he could wash away some of the mess and smell, but it only made matters worse. Now it was a sticky mess.

Arnie had written several pages of thoughts that he had had, and when and if he got back to work he would have material for a long while. The accident gave him time to write about a lot of things he'd wanted to write over the years and had put off. Maybe he wasn't as thorough as he could have been if the conditions had been different, but writing took time to think and he had plenty of that now. Sometimes he would get down in the mouth and think the future was still so uncertain that maybe this was all a waste, but if there was one thing he didn't want Julie to think happened if she made it out, was that he had given up hope. He always felt that if there was a way, Julie would find it. He just wasn't sure she had been healthy enough to do it.

It also gave him a lot of time to rethink his relationship with God, and Arnie was well on the way to becoming a born-again Christian. He hoped he lived long enough to do something about it and make his peace with God. Right now, his prayers unselfishly were more for the welfare of Julie and Timmy than for himself. He could only imagine what it had been like out in that storm last night, not knowing that they hadn't been in it.

Eetah was confused. He had followed these people for three days now, and they seemed to be in no hurry to leave the area. Two wolves from the area pack had also taken up the trailing, but Eetah handily confronted them yesterday morning and sent them running away. The wolves, an immature male and female were no match for him, and just the look and sound of his snarl make them drop their tails and slink back into the woods, but it was only a matter of time until they came back with the rest of the pack. Eetah was impressive-looking, despite his now-healed injuries, and he was also a couple of years smarter, but he'd be no match for all of them.

The pack in the area wasn't well organized, as the alpha wolf had been hurt last summer and was in danger of losing his job. As Eetah watched them, he saw the infighting and thought more than once about approaching them, but not just yet. He wanted a mate, and there would probably be one in that pack, but right now he was preoccupied with these people who had invaded his domain.

The second night that they spent on the ridge, he slept downwind only about a hundred yards away. Not really slept, but more like rested. About midnight he took some time to go hunting and had found a beaver that had wandered a long way from its creek. It took him some time to kill the beaver because it was a strong animal that he was unfamiliar with, but in the end, kill it he did, and ate his fill. He dragged the rest of the carcass to some rocks and hid it, fully intending to come back in a day or two and eat the rest.

The she creature was up again and standing on the ridge. Eetah could sense that she was in trouble, but he didn't know yet what the trouble was. He could smell her infected wound and he could detect another smell he had smelled before when he was in captivity. She was menstruating. Not that he understood what that was about, but the smell was familiar to him. The smaller one was not with her but the dog was, so he watched from a distance until she went back to her camp.

Once again Julie broke camp from the ridge, determined to get it right this time. It was a bright sunlit day, and she was going to have to make the most of it. As soon as they crossed the second ridge, Julie had a good idea where they went wrong the day before. They had walked where it was the easiest to walk, not where they needed to go.

They crossed a patch of brushy woods and broke out into a large meadow with a slough in the middle of it. They would have to go around it and this would take more time. She chose to go to the right, and that was the right decision because the walking did improve the farther along they went. They started out walking in the swamp over clumps of grass that threatened to break their ankles, but by noon they were back in the aspen trees, and a couple of hours later they were going back uphill until they reached the top of a high ridge that was mostly rock.

A fire had been through this area not too many years before and the undergrowth hadn't regenerated yet, so it made for easy walking.

This was the highest elevation in the area, and Julie could see for several miles. The land went back down into a tamarack swamp, and then there was another small ridge. She wasn't sure, but she thought she could make out a river. It was obvious they weren't going to get that far before dark, but it gave her hope and that was important. She remembered a sign her father had shown her once when she was visiting in Thunder Bay: ***This ain't the end of the world, but you can see it from here,*** and that's the way she felt at this moment..

At the edge of the ridge before it went into the tamarack forest, was a small pond, and Julie went down there to look for anything edible. Frogs, a turtle, even a snake could be eaten if you could find one. She left Timmy at the camp she'd made on the ridge about a hundred yards away, and so he could not wander away, she left Jake with him after leashing them together. Timmy was tired and hopefully he would just sit and watch her or better yet fall asleep.

She waded into the small pond and was surprised how warm the water was and how good it felt to wash up. The water was surprisingly clean, and Julie took off her clothes and washed out everything. She even washed her hair as best she could without soap. At least the mud, dust and twigs were gone.

When she was done, she put her underclothes back on and tried to catch some frogs. She did manage to get several of them. They were leopard frogs that weren't too big, but they were food, and they had to eat something. She killed the frogs, leaving them in her hard hat with some water, and brought Timmy down and bathed him, leaving the frogs to cook while they were gone.

Timmy thought it was great fun, and it seemed to lift his spirits. He'd been a real trooper, but it was rough traveling with a child. Julie knew that if she was alone she'd be at the river right now, but she wasn't alone and that was that, and she'd have to deal with it. She let Timmy run around naked for a while until he was dry, and then she put his dry clothes on him and washed the others, which were fast turning into rags.

That night the wolf pack returned and Julie could hear them howling in the distance. She hoped that they'd stay away, because she was really afraid of them. She didn't know that the only thing keeping them away right now was a wolf named Eetah, who was lying less than two hundred yards above them. He kept just far enough away to keep the dog from smelling him.

Eetah didn't know what he was going to do with these people, but something told him not to harm them, and he wasn't going to let the pack do it either. He thought about approaching the dog if he wandered far enough away, but so far he had stayed close to the people.

Julie collected quite a bit of wood, and she made the fire especially big tonight, hoping it would keep the wolves from coming close to them. She sat up late, long after Timmy went to sleep. The lump in her armpit was getting worse, and she was going to have to do something about it. She lay on her side with her head on her injured arm and probed into the wound with the small blade of Arnie's knife. She could only stand it for a second or two, and then she got squeamish and had to rest. Eventually she removed the scab and although the light from the campfire flickered so much that is was hard to see, she understood what the problem was.

There was still wood in the wound. She thought she'd removed it all, or most of it, but now she could see the end of the sliver of wood that was still in there. She was going to have to get hold of it with her fingernails and see if she could yank it out. A lot of yellowish fluid had drained out already, so it was obviously badly infected. She was able to get hold of the end of the sliver of wood but it wouldn't budge; the pain made her sick to her stomach, and she threw up the frog legs she had eaten for supper, much to Jake's delight.

On the next try it seemed like it had moved some, but she had to rest for a minute and build up some courage before trying again. She was trembling with pain and it was hard to keep her hand still. Julie gritted her teeth and, wiping the tears from her eyes so she could see the sliver, she grasped it with her thumb and forefinger and gave it one more yank.

She yelled so loud that she woke Timmy, and Jake ran a few feet away and looked at her with his ears up. Even Eetah stood up and peered through the darkness. Not only had the noise startled him, but his nose was picking up the stench of the fluid draining down her side as she sat clutching the sliver between her fingers studying it.

Julie was trembling and she moved closer to the fire. Not just for the warmth because she was shivering violently, but to more closely examine the piece of wood in the light of the fire. Timmy crawled over to her, and she put her good arm around him and held him tight. Jake still stayed about ten feet away with a puzzled look on his face.

The sliver, if you wanted to call it that, was more like the tip of a branch. It was about an inch long and some of her flesh hung from the end of it, but it also appeared as if she had gotten it all. The wound continued to drain, so Julie put her hand on the ground and leaned on the arm, hoping the slight force would keep it draining. It wasn't blood but a smelly, watery, yellow fluid that was coming out. The pressure in her shoulder was decreasing and it was feeling better already. At last she put her shirt and jacket back on and, lying down with Timmy curled up in her arms, she went to sleep. Jake wandered back and curled up at her feet, looking far beyond the fire toward the howling wolves.

In the morning her thinking was clearer and she was definitely not in as much pain as she had been. She had no food for them, and she was hungry after losing her supper, but if they got to the river she was confident she could catch more fish. The fire had burned itself out and it was cold this morning, because the temperature had dropped considerably during the night. From the warm water meeting the cold air, there was steam coming off the pond below them where she had washed Timmy and herself yesterday.

It took a while to pack everything up, but by seven-thirty they were heading out. Julie gave Timmy a lot of water to drink, thinking it would help fill him up for a while. She studied the map again, and this time looked beyond where they would meet the river. They needed to follow that river for quite a distance before it ran into another river, which eventually ran into three connecting lakes. Arnie hoped she would find people on one of these lakes, but it was going to be a few days before they got that far if they did.

Arnie had hit the beer hard and only had six bottles of that and three bottles of water left. He heard another plane this morning, but it was at the other end of the lake and it was pretty high up. It had gone north and didn't come back, so he figured that it wasn't a search plane, but someone going north to Canada.

He was also starting to feel funny. He had developed a fever, and the stink from his bottom was getting pretty bad. He must have gotten some fecal material in some sores and was getting an infection. Unlike Julie, who had performed surgery on herself, there was nothing he could do about it.

He tried to write to pass the time using shorthand to conserve on paper, but writing took research and concentration, both of which he was short on. Most of the time he just sat and imagined what it was going to look like when they did find him, just a skeleton in the seat of this airplane. Had their roles been reversed and he was the one walking out of here he would have been in Duluth by now, but Julie would be lucky if she made it out at all. This wilderness was no place for an amateur.

The next minute he would be optimistic. There had to be campers out there or someone she would find. Hell she was in good shape and Timmy was a tough kid. His problems probably were an asset in this ordeal. Timmy really never worried about anything.

It had been over a week now since they disappeared. Back at the bank the flowers had wilted and then vanished from Julie's desk, and one of the other tellers had taken her position. There was talk of a memorial service, but not everybody had given up on them, especially not Irv, who was back searching almost every day. He hadn't had much luck with any other volunteers flying and searching, but he never had had much hope for extra help from the start. People had jobs and responsibilities.

The Department of Natural Resources had instructed their pilots to keep their eyes open, but that was about all they could do. Arnie's mom had stubbornly refused to give up her post, but finally left the porch and retreated into the house where it was warmer. Irv came out every other day to check on her and bring her food and cigarettes.

At the newspaper they reran some of Arnie's old columns, but if they didn't hear from him by the following week, they were planning to use his space for something else. Shirley had given him and the family up for lost, and was blaming herself because she was the one who talked him into the new plane. She figured that Arnie hadn't been ready to fly that plane yet, and that was what had gotten him into trouble. The assistant editor was running things while, for the first time that people at the paper could remember, Shirley stayed home. She had no idea when she would be back and told them to leave her alone, she would come back when she was ready to come back She left the house only to get more booze and cigarettes and she called Irv at least once a day for news. So far she had wired him over a thousand dollars to keep flying.

CHAPTER 11

▼

Tamarack forests are relentless at keeping people from walking through them. They grow practically into an impenetrable barrier. Their branches intertwine and reach all the way to the ground like a thick hedge. That, and the fact that Julie and Timmy were back in the swamp again made the going rough, and at times they were reduced to almost crawling. They had been cold this morning, but the exertion from fighting the brush and the swamp had Julie sweating hard before they traveled even a mile. It didn't help that she literally had to drag Timmy along. He was hungry and tired, and wanted no part of going anywhere.

Jake, who normally hunted everywhere he went, was now content to bring up the rear. He hadn't eaten food for three days except Julie's supper of frog legs that she had tossed up, and it was taking a toll on him. His coat was full of brambles, and the pads on one of his front feet were cut, leaving bloody prints on the rocks as he walked.

Eetah followed less than a quarter mile behind them. He could smell the blood in Jake's paw print, and his senses again told him they were in trouble. There were times during the day that he could hear Timmy's cries when he fought with Julie. They had left the area that the wolf pack claimed, and they were in danger now of getting into a new pack's area. The next one might not be as unorganized as the last one. Eetah succeeded in keeping the last group away, but he would be no match for a well-organized pack. He couldn't get over the fact that this type of people had helped him once, and he would like to return the favor, but right now he didn't know what to do, and he was also still suspicious of Jake.

Julie was feeling defeated. From the ridge this morning, she could make out the meandering river. The tamarack swamp between them and the river hadn't looked this inhospitable, but it was becoming nearly impossible to move forward. She tied a T-shirt around Timmy's head to keep the branches out of his face. Her own face was crisscrossed with cuts and scratches, as were her arms. Her jeans had been reduced to rags, and there were hardly any leggings left on them. Her shoelaces were broken, and she was continually stopping to pull her shoes from the muck that threatened to not only pull them off, but to swallow them up for good. Her jacket was in tatters and she was exhausted.

Julie lost all sense of direction in the swamp, and for all she knew they would end up back where they started, or worse yet; wander around in this god-forsaken place until they died of exhaustion. She had tried the cell phone once more when she was high on the ridge before they left this morning, but it was dead. In a fit of anger, she threw it away. She had enough dead or dying things to worry about, she didn't need that one too. She was feeling very despondent and overcome.

Shortly after noon before they stopped to rest alongside a small pond. She was too tired to fish for food, if there was any in it, but she was able to catch a few more frogs and some minnows in her shirt by laying it on the bottom and using it like a sieve. She held the lighter up to the light and could barely make out the fluid left in the bottom. It had very few lights left in it, and she had no idea what she would do when it ran dry. The only thing she could do was make sure she got her fires started as quickly as possible.

After they finished eating their meager meal, Julie noticed that the pond they were at had a current, so they walked to the other end of it and saw it was emptying into a small stream. She sat down and studied her map. It didn't show every little stream and creek, and it did not show this one either. There were a few little fingers of water that drained from the swamp and they eventually drained into the river. Then it hit her. They only needed to follow the stream. It had to go to the river. That's what streams and creeks do.

It was hard walking along the side of the stream, so they waded for the most part. The water was cold, and they had to get out occasionally to warm up their feet, but at least there was no brush slapping their faces, and she was confident that they were at least heading in the right direction.

As they went along, Julie noticed that other streams emptied into the one they were walking in. It was getting wider and a few spots were nearly up to her waist, so they had to get out and walk around them. For a while she carried Timmy on her back, as she didn't want him getting any wetter than necessary, but that proved too exhausting, especially with all their possessions rolled up in the tarp that she had to tied onto his back, so they returned to the water walking hand in hand, he would just have to get wet. Jake took turns running on shore and then jumping in to swim for a while.

Hunger was starting to gnaw at Julie's insides, and she was out of energy. Several times she stumbled and fell in the water, but she plodded on until suddenly she could hear the river in the distance. It was obvious, from the sound of the rushing water, that it was not a small river.

They needed to set up camp and rest soon. She told herself that she would catch some fish for supper, and then everything would be all right. Her spirits were getting a little brighter.

They came to a large beaver dam, so they had to leave the creek bed once again and walk on land. As Julie walked, she noticed the woods were thinning out. It was more trees, less brush, and less swamp, and they were making a lot better time. They came over a small rise and there it was in front of her, the mighty Sawbuck River. It was about one hundred feet wide and the current was swift and looked treacherous. The river was full of rocks, and the banks were also lined with rocks that had survived years of rampaging water making its way south to Heron Lake. Arnie had told her that no boats ever used the Sawbuck because it was just too wild, and what she saw now gave testament to that statement.

Julie decided they would stay where they were for the night, so she made camp and wrapped Timmy in the blanket, getting him to sleep with the medicine, which was nearly depleted, then she and Jake went down to the river to fish. They weren't in a good spot for fishing as the water was too swift, so they walked downstream about five hundred feet to where the river made a bend and seemed to flatten out a little. Timmy was sleeping now and she hoped he would stay asleep, because she didn't want to move him, even though she would hear him, she couldn't see him from where she was. She was just too tired and hungry to even think straight.

Eetah came across the boy almost by accident. He had trailed them all day and lay in the woods while the she-person made camp. He saw her and the dog leave, and he walked around the camp to follow them when his nose told him that the shelter wasn't empty. He circled from twenty feet away, his nose testing the air with every step. It was only the child that he smelled. He could hear the boy's ragged breathing in the shelter, and he approached him cautiously.

The refuge consisted of canvas draped over a fallen tree, which was a few feet off the ground and supported by several limbs. Julie had put some wood on the back part of the canvas to hold it down, but the front side was open to the elements. Timmy was sleeping with his back to the back of the shelter, wrapped in their only blanket, with only his head and neck showing. His hair was matted into greasy curls, and his face was smeared with mud and streaked where tears had run down his cheeks.

Eetah crept forward on his haunches, until he was just inches from the boy's face. He could smell the boy's rancid breath and could detect the hunger that was there. Slowly and methodically, he licked Timmy's face and hair lightly until he was clean, and then he sat down beside him. He would find them food just as his father had done when he was a young pup in the pack.

Julie fished for several hours with no luck at all. She managed to hook only one fish and it had broken her line and stolen her best lure. With darkness closing in, she filled their water bottles and walked back to the camp, dejected and hungry. Timmy was her big worry. Somehow she had to find food for him, as huger made him unmanageable. In Timmy's state of mind, all discomforts made him unmanageable. She also realized that if she didn't eat something herself, she would not be able to function much longer either.

Eetah had heard them coming and slipped back into the forests, but not undetected. Jake, hungry and weak as he was, could smell the wolf's scent and recognized it as an intruder. He ran from the camp in several directions, barking at his unseen opponent to let him know he was still capable of protecting his friends.

Julie was curious about Jake's behavior, but chalked it up to a squirrel or a raccoon, two of Jake's favorite animals to pester. She made a fire noting how little the flame was on the lighter, and lay down next to Timmy to go to sleep. She ran her fingers through his hair, and then suddenly sat up and looked at him in the light from the campfire. His hair was wet and his face was clean, not the way he had been when she put him down to sleep. Jake would not stop smelling Timmy's hair and growling. What was going on here?

By the time Jake finished throwing his fit; Eetah was a half a mile away. He hunted best in the dark, and tonight was a perfect night for hunting. He hadn't come across any scent patches for a while, so it was possible that no other wolves had claimed this territory. Maybe it would be his if things worked out and he found a mate.

Almost any warm-blooded creature in the forest would make a good meal for a wolf, but tonight he was looking for something special. He had a taste for venison. There were a lot of deer in the woods, but most of the time they smelled him as easily as he smelled them and then they were long gone. Wolves are very successful hunting in packs, but hunting by oneself was a special challenge.

Eetah stood on a small ridge and tested the air for scent. There was not much wind tonight, but he could smell a deer maybe a mile away, and if the conditions were right, and they had never been better than tonight, he just might be successful. The scent was coming from the river, and he approached it cautiously from downwind. He circled around and locked in on it, being very careful not to make any noise, as he crept along the riverbank, keeping the wind into his face he saw them, a doe and two fawns drinking at the water's edge. He knew he couldn't catch the doe, but the fawns were a different story. He would sneak in as close as he could and then charge them. They wouldn't want to go in the river, so he figured they would run away from him upstream.

The doe made a big mistake. Her nose didn't detect the wolf until he was only about fifty yards from them. It took her a few seconds to figure out which way to escape, and by then Eetah was only fifty feet away and closing in at a full sprint. She went to her right with the fawns close behind, but it was too late, and she heard the bones break in the little fawns back as Eetah attacked him. There was nothing she could do but save herself and her other fawn. They took flight, passing within fifty feet of Julie's camp.

Jake had heard the deer go by but it was quiet now, and he lay back down with a growl that Eetah heard a quarter a mile away. Eetah ate his fill and then dragged the remains as close to the camp as he could without alarming Jake. Then he went into the woods to find a place to sleep.

The sores on Arnie's butt were infected, and the acid in the beer was only making things worse. He was unaware of the fact that his kidneys were starting to fail from the toxins in his infections. Without proper medical treatment, he wouldn't survive many more days. He had a high fever, and he was slipping in and out of consciousness. A massive infection like this would be hard to manage in a hospital with the best of care.

He was starting to imagine things, like other planes flying over, and boats on the lake, and it frustrated him that no one would stop and help. One minute he was praying to God, and the next he was cursing the fact that God had made them crash in this desolate place, *blasting his beautiful plane with that bolt of lightning.* He could hear noises under the plane and was convinced it was Julie. He was sure she hadn't left yet and was ignoring him and humoring him.

Didn't she realize they would all die here if she didn't get her ass in gear and find someone to help them? he wondered out loud. *Julie, damn it, come here. I want to talk to you. I gave you a map and told you how to get out of here, and all you do is fuck around under this plane. This isn't any joking matter. I know you're pissed off because I crashed, but that's no damn reason to behave like this Julie, do you hear me? Do you hear me, Julie? You spoiled little shit.* He pounded his fist on the dash of the plane.

Arnie quieted down and thought again about writing the letter to Julie, but his emotions were so mixed up right now it was hard to think. His mind was playing games with him and he knew it. He was ashamed for being mad at her and knew that she was doing all that she could.

His thoughts went back to another day and another place. He and Julie were walking down a country road that was just a lane in the bright summer sunlight, holding hands and stopping from time to time to embrace. She was so pretty that day. She had worn a bright yellow sundress with thin straps, and sandals that flopped on her feet when she walked. Her shoulders were freckled from the sun and her hair was bleached out to an almost orange color. They had gone to a quiet pond and sat on the shore feeding some baby ducks part of the bread from the sandwiches that she made. That was the day that they had made the decision to live together. She told him how much she loved him and Timmy. They had made love right there in the warm sand by the edge of the pond, then swam together in the warm water clinging to each other as if they were one. There was no way they could get enough of each other. Arnie smiled gently as a tear slid down his cheek and disappeared in his beard. He remembered that day so vividly, and then the fogginess came rushing back and he lapsed into unconsciousness.

CHAPTER 12

▼

When Julie woke up, Jake was gone. It was unusual for him to stray, but hunger was driving him to be bolder. Even though his sense of smell was nowhere close to Eetah's, it was still very keen and he awakened to the smell of fresh meat. He cautiously approached the deer kill, and not finding any competition, he moved in. The only part of the deer that had been eaten was the stomach cavity, most likely the liver and heart. This was a small deer; this year's fawn, and Eetah could have easily eaten the whole thing if he wanted to. Jake could smell Eetah's scent on the deer, but his hunger was too intense, and he started chewing on a hind quarter before Julie's calls and whistles got his attention.

He ran partway back to where Julie could see him, but he didn't want to leave his newfound food source, so he stood and whined. Julie could see bloodstains on his face and chest and walked toward him cautiously. Jake ran back to his food cache and stood over it, growling at Julie, while his tail wagged furiously. She petted the big dog and settled him down as she inspected the kill. Had Jake killed this deer? Its back was broken and there was still steam coming from the insides. *My God,* She thought. *Jake was feeding them. What a dog!*

She hauled the deer back to the campsite and hung it up with the rope. She and Arnie had dressed a lot of deer, so she knew just what to do. She found some more firewood and got a big fire going to cook the venison. First, though, she was going to cook a small steak for breakfast. Jake was still looking at her with a quizzical look that said, *Hey, that's mine.*

Timmy woke up crying from hunger, but the warm meat soon satisfied him and he settled down after eating. Julie worked as fast as she could to process the rest of the meat and get it cooked.

At the wolf center north of Duluth, Tom Bobson and Laurie Cross were going through their preflight check before they went out to look for wolves that had transmitting collars on them. Tom and Laurie had both been biology students at the University in Duluth and worked for the state to supplement their incomes while going to school. After graduation they both stayed on to work on the wolf program, which Laurie was especially interested in.

She was an intense person who was all business from the moment she got to work.

She worked with Tom a lot and their relationship had always been cordial and professional, even though Tom was just the opposite of Laurie. He was more free spirited and liked to party at night in the waterfront bars and cafes. He was short and built like a linebacker, with big shoulders and a broad back. He was also a fearless pilot, who despite his young age knew how to handle himself in an aircraft. Tom was also qualified to fly helicopters.

He loved to push Laurie's buttons when she got too serious about things, but she knew that and played along with him. He talked about quitting and moving to Alaska in the spring and she hoped he wouldn't. Tom wanted to be a bush pilot.

They would find as many wolves as they were able and note their location on a large grid they had made that showed their migrating habits as they wandered around the wilderness. They did this once a month, and on most occasions found the general percentage of the animals that were in the program.

For some of the wolves, this would be their last check as the batteries were going dead in their collars, and Eetah was one of them. They found him last month by his transmitter, but they didn't see him, because he stayed hidden in the underbrush. Laurie was one of the people who had made contact with Eetah when he was captured, and she would love to see him again. He was a magnificent specimen, and she wished there was some way they could change the batteries in his collar, but that didn't seem possible right now. The helicopter flights that it took to capture them and the sleep tranquilizers were expensive, and money was short, so they were saving those flights for mercy missions only. This would be day one in their attempt to locate the wolves, and it usually took about three days before they found them all, or gave up. Today they would search an area north of Duluth along the lakeshore and tomorrow they would head west of there. The area that Eetah and Julie were in was south of that area, on the fringe. The area where Arnie was lying was smack in the middle of it.

Arnie had suffered through a bad night, his body racked with fever from the infection invading his body. When his back had been broken, he had lost all sensation below his chest, but for some reason he didn't lose the sensations to his internal organs and still had his bladder and bowel function. In regard to his bladder function, he learned to relieve himself without wetting himself, but his bowel function could not be controlled, and although he had held it for several days, there came a time when he could hold it no longer. The acids in his waste had eaten away at his soft tissue on his buttocks, causing sores that were now infected. His liquid diet helped to not accumulate much waste, but as he got sicker he developed diarrhea, which only made him more miserable.

Today Arnie's fever was 103, and he was having difficulty focusing his vision or having an attention span of more than a few seconds on any one subject. He drank his last beer yesterday and then threw it back up a few minutes later. This only added to the mess he was in.

Even the squirrel that had been living in the seat cushion deserted him because of the stench.

He thought about Julie, but only in brief episodes. It was like she had deserted him, and he didn't know why. He thought of Timmy, but had not thought of him being with Julie. Maybe his mom had come and gotten him. Not Arnie's mom, Timmy's mom, Ann. He hadn't thought of her for a long time. He had promised her that he would always do what was best for their son. *What the hell was she doing back here anyway? Sticking her nose where it didn't belong.*

If he was going to write Julie a letter, in case he didn't get out of here, maybe today should be the day before he went completely nuts Arnie thought in a moment of lucidity. He searched around the plane for his pad of paper. Where the hell had he put that now? It wasn't like he could have left it anywhere else. At last he saw it on the dash of the plane. There were only a few pages left that were blank. He turned to the last one, which was reserved with the heading, *My Dearest Julie.* But before he wrote, he was going to close his eyes for a few minutes and think about what he wanted to say. Closing his eyes for those few minutes was all it took for Arnie to fall asleep.

Julie used up most of the day by cooking the deer meat and putting it in the plastic bag she had brought it with her. The cooked meat would not spoil so fast now and should last them for a few days at least. It was probably too late to start moving today, and she felt bad about that. Arnie's food supply had to be low by now, and every day was important for his survival.

She gave Jake a good sized piece of meat. After all, it was his kill. She still had trouble getting used to the idea that Jake had killed a deer and eaten the liver and the heart before she took it away from him. Maybe he was a better hunter than she gave him credit for.

Eetah had hoped to lure Jake away from Julie with the deer kill and it almost worked. He wasn't far away when Jake found the deer and started eating, and he was actually moving in on Jake when Julie's voice, calling the dog had sent him scurrying away. He was now about a quarter of a mile away, resting on a hillside covered with heavy grass. He had just finished eating part of a woodchuck that was a little late getting into its burrow, and now he was cleaning up his fur and doing a little grooming in the fall sun. Maybe tonight he would try to get close to the camp again. Suddenly a scent that he thought he recognized came across the hillside, and he stood up and tried to orient himself as to where it was coming from.

She had left her pack a week ago to look for a mate. She was a year younger than Eetah and quite a bit smaller, but she too was an excellent hunter. Right now she wasn't hunting for food; she too was hunting for a companion. She didn't smell Eetah, but he smelled her, and he rose and trotted downwind from her. He moved as stealthily as a cat until he spotted her drinking from the river. The wind was coming from across the river and she didn't smell him until he was within thirty feet of her, and then she whirled, baring her teeth as she growled at him. She wasn't in season yet, but it wouldn't be long, and it was this smell that Eetah had been most drawn to. Her growling stopped and she relaxed her mouth so her fangs didn't show. She stood motionlessly, staring at Eetah, who was also frozen in place. Slowly and cautiously, they circled each other in an ever-tightening circle until they were just a few feet apart. Eetah was magnificent and was all that she had been looking for, but she had some questions yet. Was he part of a pack? She sensed no other wolves nearby. She tried to approach the pack that Eetah was following the day before but had been chased off. There was still a bite mark on her ear from that encounter.

At last they were nose to nose, and Eetah licked her face and cautiously lowered himself to his haunches. It was his way of saying, *at ease, little woman. Everything will be fine.* They inspected each other's bodies, and then they frolicked in the warmth of the late afternoon sun. Eetah took her to what was left of the half-eaten woodchuck that he had for lunch, and she hungrily finished off the rest. Then they went downstream from where Julie was camped and lay down together on the riverbank for a nap.

According to the map Julie had spread out before her, they were about three days from Heron Lake. Once again the land was low and brushy, so it was going to be hard traveling. Worse, there was no reason to believe they would be rescued immediately when they reached the lake. People did not live there. It was just a great camping lake, but it was late in the year and … *oh hell, she had to get to Heron Lake first and worry about who or who wasn't there later.*

It hadn't rained for a few days and the weather was unseasonably warm, but now the clouds were thickening, and she could feel the temperature dropping. She and Timmy had put on all the clothes they had with them and now only had to carry their one blanket, the blue tarp, the fishing pole in its case with the map, and her fire-blackened hard hat. If she ever got out of here, she was thinking about starting a line of cookware using tin hats. Tonight was a better night for a change. They weren't hungry, and she knew the way to Heron Lake.

Julie had fallen asleep early, so she was awake before dawn and anxious to get going. Before she got up she counted the days they had been gone from Arnie. This had to be day six. He couldn't have much food or water left and that bothered her. For the first time she thought about all the people who would be missing them, like her parents and Arnie's mom. She knew Irv would have been concerned, and she wondered who else? Then she sat up shaking her head and thinking. For she couldn't let that concern her. That kind of talk only would distract her.

What did concern her, however, was her personal hygiene. She had always been fastidious about her cleanliness, and prided herself on her appearance. She didn't have a mirror to look in, but she must be a mess judging from what she could see and smell. If only she had some warm water to wash in, even if she had no soap.

She heard wolves during the night, but it didn't sound like a lot of them. It was more like just a couple, but they sounded close. Jake was so upset that he had spent half the night growling. She was proud of the fact that they didn't alarm her so much anymore.

It was back to reality. They chewed some cold venison before they stepped out into the soggy weather and headed downstream. It was raining just hard enough to make things miserable. Julie tried to hold the tarp around them to keep them dry, but the brush kept snagging it and pulling it away.

Around noon she found some more wild rice, and she wrapped Timmy in the tarp while she harvested another hatful. They would have rice with their venison for supper tonight and what a feast it would be.

They pushed on through the afternoon, trying to stay close to the riverbank but having to retreat from time to time, as the brush was too thick in many places. They were about three hundred feet from the river when Julie saw something that looked out of place. It was close to the river bank, and cautiously she went to investigate. She couldn't believe her eyes until she stood only a few feet from it. It was a cabin, or had been a cabin at one time. The front door was hanging by one hinge and all the glass was gone from the windows. Looking inside she saw that some of the floorboards had rotted away. She was looking at the ground underneath and the skeletal remains of the supports. The roof had fallen inside so no one could get into the back half of the building. A birch clump was growing inside the cabin and its limbs were poking out of the roofline. At one time there had been a huge rock fireplace. Although some of it had crumbled away, most of it was still intact, including some pine logs that had been split in half for a mantle. Most of the chinking was gone from between the logs in the walls, and light was streaming in through the open spaces. Outside, the logs on the north and east sides were covered with dark green moss and some kind of wild vine was growing up the backside of the cabin.

She walked around to the back, where the remnants of some kind of outbuilding, most likely a privy, had given up and collapsed into the hole it had serviced. There were several rusted-out coffee and lard cans, along with a pile of beer bottles stacked alongside the remains of the building. A little farther into the woods were two barrels that were more holes than metal and looked like they had been containers for something at one time.

Julie stood and stared for a few minutes. Someone had lived here at one time. Someone had sought the peace and solitude of the forest in which to spend their life. But where were they now? It was time to call it a day, and maybe they would stay here tonight. It wasn't much of a cabin, but it was better than nothing, and that's what they had right now: nothing.

They went inside, being careful where they stepped, and found a section of floor big enough to lay their gear on. What roof that was left sheltered this area, so at least it was dry. Julie started a fire in the fireplace with the last bit of fluid in the lighter. She put it back in her pocket just in case it regenerated itself and actually worked once more, but it looked empty. The flame was so low she was lucky to get the dry grass she'd brought in lit before the flame went out.

It was a long night with little rest for Julie. She cooked up some rice and venison for supper, and they ate all they wanted. She also had to boil the drinking water now because the river water was less than clean. The old hard hat was not going to survive many more meals and was not recognizable any longer as a hard hat.

Having no way to start another fire, Julie was concerned about the fire going out, so she was up every couple of hours to add more wood. She tried to think of some way to bring coals with them in the morning to start another fire, but the hard hat was the only container they had, and she wasn't going to be able to carry it with hot coals inside. The sound of the wolves still bothered her, and she felt that fire was the only defense they had. They were howling again, and Jake growled and tested the air several times inside, but was reluctant to go outside. Julie lay on the small piece of flooring with Timmy in her arms and watched the fire flickering in the fireplace. She wondered what it had been like to live here so many years ago. She also wondered who had lived here at one time. Had it been a trapper, or was it someone who just wanted to get away from it all? There were no possessions in the cabin that gave any indication as to who or why. Just before dark, she got up and went outside and walked a few yards behind the cabin to relieve herself. Sitting on a log while she took care of business, she saw a small marker a few yards away and went to inspect it. It was two logs fashioned into the form of a cross and she could barely make out the words that had been carved into the top log. She could faintly read the words, **Allison Edison, Died June 4th, 1933, age 9**. A family had lived here nearly seventy years ago and it was in the thirties, not the middle 1800's. Why were they living way out here, and whatever happened to the rest of them? She knelt by the grave and thought of the little girl who was buried here. What kind of life did she have out in this god forsaken country?

Suddenly Timmy's screams brought her back out of her dream world, and she raced to the doorway of the cabin with Jake right behind her. Timmy stood with his back to the wall and pointed to the hole in the floor where a black animal with a long white stripe down its back stood looking at him. It was a skunk and he was as scared as Timmy was. When he saw Julie, he beat a hasty retreat back under the flooring worried the Jake might follow him. Julie grabbed him but the big Lab had already had one bad encounter with a skunk back home, and he had no intention of going after this one.

She took Timmy in her arms and rocked and hummed to him to settle him down. Then they both lay down to go to sleep. *I wish we had a boat*, she though to herself. *That river is flowing the way we want to go, and it sure would beat walking.* But she might as well wish for a leather couch to sleep on while she was wishing. Her grandmother used to say, "If wishes were horses, then beggars would ride." Now she finally knew what that dear old woman meant. At that moment her eyes fell on the heavy door that hung by one hinge. Maybe a raft? Could that work? With that thought, she fell asleep.

CHAPTER 13

▼

Today was a big day for them … no more damn walking. Julie had lugged the heavy door down to the river's edge and it floated like the Queen Mary. It would need a little something added to it for buoyancy, but that was easily fixed by using the logs that had been over the fireplace mantel and the rope she had been lugging along. She also devised a way to pack the hard hat in mud on the raft to keep her fire going. There wasn't going to be room for Jake, but he could run the river bank alongside them. She also found a long pole that she could use for steering the craft. They would try to stay close to the bank where the water wasn't too deep.

The river was flowing fast, but for the most part it was not that wild, and definitely could not be called 'white water.' It was from four to five feet deep on average, but there were stretches where it was much deeper, and other places where it was dotted with frequent sandbars. The winding river had been cutting its course through the bedrock for centuries, and in many places the banks rose several feet above the water level, even though the water was high right now.

Julie could not get the image of the grave out of her mind as she finished tying up the raft and making preparations to leave. She knew that if she got out of here and back to civilization, she was going to find out more about the people who had once lived here, and what happened to them. They had a good breakfast of rice and meat, got aboard the raft, and shoved off. The current quickly took them, and the cabin disappeared from their sight. It was clear and sunny, although it seemed to be getting colder each day.

After all of her trials and tribulations, Julie's spirits had rebounded and she now had more hope that they were going to make it out of here. They had a ways to go, but maybe God had heard her prayers and was keeping an eye on them. It seemed that when things got worse they always found a way out of it and something would come along and ease their plight. She said a silent prayer of thanks

Arnie was unconscious now more than he was awake. His body was racked with fever, and he had drunk the last of his water this morning. If someone didn't get to him in the next day or so, he was not going to make it, as dehydrations would take its toll, but he didn't realize this himself, as he had little reasoning ability left.

He wanted to write that last letter to Julie, because it now appeared that he was not going to leave here alive, but he just couldn't get his mind to function well enough to even find his pencil which was in his pocket, and his paper which was in his lap, let alone write something that would make sense.

There were times when, for a few minutes, his mind would clear and he could think rationally again, and the next time that that happened he was going to have to take advantage of it. That is, if it did happen again. His moods changed from hour to hour from being mad at Julie, to missing her. Right now he was thinking about Shirley Capes and what a good person she was. *She was going to be mad when she heard what he did to her plane,* he thought. *'No wait, it was his plan ... e or was it? Shit, he had to think about that.*

This was the second day of the over-flight to find and track the collared wolves. Yesterday Tom and Laurie had been successful in finding most of them. They experienced some sadness when one of the wolves was spotted dead on the shore of a small lake. From the air it appeared to be the result of a fight. They had GPS coordinates and would follow it up with a helicopter flight in the next few days. Both Tom and Laurie were pilots, but Tom did most of the flying in the plane and the helicopter, while Laurie handled the instruments. She was too interested in her work to worry about flying. Yesterday they had lost a day, because fog had settled in and kept the airport closed.

Today they would be much closer to Eetah's area than they were before, but still would probably not get that far south. If they had a good day today, they might call it quits early and go retrieve the dead wolf before something happened to his body.

Eetah was enjoying his newfound friendship with the young female wolf, but still he was not going to leave these people alone until they left the area. His companion trusted him enough to tag along, but she stayed a long way back. Last night they slept curled around each other for part of the night, and then had successfully killed an old sick doe and gorged on it. Instinct told them that they needed to eat well while they could because winter was coming, the hunting would be harder, and food would be scarce.

They came to the cabin just as Julie was leaving on the raft them from the shelter of the woods. The woman and the boy left without the dog.

Jake was separated from Julie and Timmy but he knew they were out there. He was very nervous. He ran along the bank for a while, and then he jumped in and started swimming for the raft. Julie stayed close to the shore and she yelled at Jake to go back, but he was having no part of it. Jake smelled the wolves and he was terrified. He tried to climb aboard the raft, so Julie took Timmy to the opposite side so he wouldn't swamp them. As hard as the dog tried, he was not going to get on without some help, and Julie was not able to help him without tipping them. His efforts soon tired him out, and he swam along side, rather than going back to shore. It was more like he floated with the current. The big dog was a swimming machine; his heavy oily coat trapped air inside of it and made him buoyant. It also kept the cold water from getting to his skin.

They went on for about a mile like this, and then the raft went into some shallow water, and Jake was able to touch bottom. With help from Julie, the tired dog was finally able to get aboard the raft, and they started off again. They were making good time, and she figured with any luck at all they would reach Heron Lake sometime tomorrow.

It was so nice not to be walking and getting slapped with brush and stickers. They still had some meat left, and Julie was going to catch a fish this afternoon; she had made up her mind about that. Timmy seemed to be content with the raft riding, but Julie was having some problems getting him to sit still. She tethered him to Jake's collar, because Jake was good about staying in place. They were cold because they weren't moving around, but they still had the small fire in the helmet, which she kept going with scraps of wood she brought along and they warmed their hands over it from time to time.

Eetah and his friend followed the raft's progress for a while, but they too were getting tired of all the running through the brush, and decided to head inland to find a place for a nap and to let their big meal from this morning settle. Maybe it was time to leave these people alone and put a claim on some territory if they were going to start a pack of their own. This did seem to be undisputed land they were in. He hadn't found any scent patches for two days now.

Julie had her back to the river, talking to Timmy, and never saw the rock they hit until it was too late. All she knew was that she was catapulted backward over the rock and into the river. She remembered going down, her back scraping the bottom, and kicking with all her might to get free of the current. An undertow in front of the rock would not let go of her. Her mind was turning blank and her strength was leaving her, when, as quickly as it had grabbed her, the current spit her back out. She bobbed to the surface. For a second she didn't realize she was free, and then her starved lungs could hold out no more. She sucked in air and water as she came afloat and saw the next rock in front of her. She reached out and grabbed the branch of a deadhead that was lodged in it. The water was unbelievably cold, and she knew she had to get out of it as soon as possible.

She held on for her life, and carefully hand over hand, worked her way up the branch and onto the rock. It was then that two things came to her mind at once, Timmy and Jake. Where were they? She stood up as much as her strength would let her and screamed, "Timmy!" She looked downstream. The raft was empty and floating rapidly away. The water was rough enough here that she wasn't looking at a flat surface of water any longer. It was more like a white-capped lake. There was no sign of Timmy, and Julie's heart lurched as she realized what had happened. A loud involuntary moan came from her throat, followed by a scream. She fell to her knees on the rock, sobbing, but as she raised her head to scream again, she saw Jake pulling himself up onto the river bank, with Timmy behind him. Timmy's hand was still tied to his collar.

Julie didn't even think about what she was doing. The shoreline was about seventy-five feet away, and she dove in and swam with all her strength. The current carried her quite a distance downstream, but she eventually pulled herself onto the muddy shoreline and fell, exhausted, but not quitting.

She was on her knees trying to think. Timmy ... where was he? He had been with Jake but where did they go? She had to get back to Timmy. She stood and ran a few feet and fell back into the river. Pulling herself back out, she climbed over the bank this time and made her way upstream through the brush. She had lost her shoes, shirt, and jacket, torn away by the rocks and current. Her tattered jeans and bra were all she had left for clothing, but right now Timmy was all she could think of.

Jake was barking and she followed the noise until she saw him struggling across the ground, pulling Timmy behind him. Julie fell to the ground, picked Timmy up in her arms, and put her lips to his to blow air into his mouth. His lips were blue and his shoulder was dislocated from being dragged through the river by the dog, but he was alive. He was moaning and breathing and Julie rocked back and forth, holding him and crying harder than she had ever cried before in her life. It was then that she realized how cold she was and how little she had left on. Timmy had also lost one shoe and his clothes were in worse shape than hers. Everything had been going so well and now this. It seemed like this was the last straw.

There was a large log a few feet away, and Julie pulled Timmy into her arms, carried him over to it and they both laid down next to the log, with her body shielding his from the wind. His eyes were open and he started to cry and Julie talked to him and rubbed his back and arms until he settled down. The temperature was about forty degrees and they were both shivering violently. Now they had nothing. No dry clothes. No tarp. No fire in their beloved hard hat. No fishing rod. No food. They were going to die and that was all there was to it. Julie tried to warm Timmy as much as she could with what heat was left in her body. She was so tired but she mustn't go to sleep. *But why not? They were going to die anyway.* She had been so upbeat this morning, but now it seemed their luck had run out. Was this the end?

Jake came and lay down next to Julie. He too was exhausted, but he wasn't as cold. He tried to shelter her with his body. It was nearly dark now and he could smell the familiar scent of the wolves. They weren't that far away.

Julie's mind was fogging over. She dreamt she was back behind the cabin, and there were now two new crosses next to the old one. Hers and Timmy's, and there were new fresh mounds of dirt. Jake was lying on top of the one grave with her name carved into the cross, and. Arnie sat on the log where she once had sat, crying for both of them.

Eetah had heard Julie's scream and turned back to the river. His mate followed, although reluctantly. She couldn't figure out why he didn't either attack these people or leave them alone. Simply tracking them was a waste of energy.

Eetah was trotting at a brisk pace, as if he knew there was some sort of urgency for him to find them. His nose already had them in range, however, and he slowed down as he got close enough to see them. He could make out Jake's head, as Jake too was testing the air.

Jake was terrified now. He couldn't leave Julie and Timmy, as much as he wanted to run away, and he knew that he was no match for these two wolves. Jake cowered behind Julie as Eetah came closer, until no more than a few feet separated the two of them. There was no aggression in Eetah's face, and maybe it was the fact that they both belonged to the wolf family that brought a bit of a bond to both of them. This was no time to fight. Jake rolled onto his side and exposed his belly to the wolf. Eetah stood over Jake and looked down on him before he also lay down next to Julie.

Eetah's mate was still a hundred yards back and wanted no part of this. She settled on top of a mound of dirt and watched. Eetah started licking Julie's face and hair, and then turned to Timmy and did the same. Timmy was still conscious and although he didn't seem to be afraid, he was not moving, just staring at the big wolf with wide-open eyes.

Julie's heartbeat was slowing and her body temperature had dropped to a critical point. Without care, she wouldn't live long.

Tom Bobson was calling it a day. It was getting dark and they hadn't picked up any signals all day. It was his bowling night and he wanted to get back. His whistle was dry, and cold beer and hamburgers sounded real good. He reached over and tapped Laurie on the shoulder to get her attention as the noise from the engine made talking difficult.

Laurie was bent over her screen and didn't respond to his shoulder tap until he repeated it. "I have a signal," she shouted and pointed to the screen.

"Pretty late," Tom said.

"This one is close. Let's get it first, and then head out of here. If it's who I think it is, we'll be done anyway, and I don't want to come back tomorrow for just this one signal."

It was Laurie's call. She was in charge of the program, so Tom changed course and they locked in on the signal. They were over the north end of Borden Lake, and the signal seemed to be coming from just a few miles north of that. There had never been wolves this far south that he knew of, but they liked to wander, and it would be a good sign for a new pack to start in this area. When they came to the river on the north end of the lake, Laurie asked Tom to drop down and follow the river for a while. The signal was getting stronger just ahead of them. He dropped the plane down to just a few feet over the water.

Directly below them, she spotted a small raft floating in the river and there was smoke coming from it, although it appeared to be empty. There was also a blue tarp rolled up on the raft, and Laurie asked Tom to circle and take another look at it. By the time Tom could turn around, he was a couple more miles north, and he brought the plane down to fifty feet above the water this time. He just wanted to get out of here.

The signal, which Laurie had forgotten about for the moment, now seemed to be right below them. Her eyes scanned the river, but it was Tom looking out the other window who saw the big wolf standing over Julie. He was speechless for a second, and then tapped Laurie's back once more, pointing to the area while he brought the plane around again.

This time Laurie saw it too. In fact, she saw more than Tom had seen. She saw the wolf, Julie, Timmy, and Jake, and could hardly believe her eyes. Tom brought the plane around again and they made one more pass as low as they could. They grabbed the radio off the dash. "This is D and R six-four-two to Duluth base," he called.

"Go ahead, six-four-two." The base responded.

"We have spotted some people who seem to be in trouble up on the Sawbuck River. Need a rescue chopper immediately. Do you copy?"

"We copy, six-four-two. How do you know they are in trouble?"

"They are unresponsive and surrounded by wolves," Tom radioed back.

CHAPTER 14

▼

The rescue helicopter had to come out of the Coast Guard base in Duluth as regular Medivac choppers from the hospitals wouldn't be able to land in the woods and brush. Tom and Laurie continued to circle the area. They saw movement from the dog and the wolf, but no sign of life from the people. Even after dark they continued to circle until they saw the lights from the incoming chopper. It was a full moon night, so for the time being they did have some visibility, but the signal from the wolf's collar was the main thing they locked in on. A huge cloudbank was approaching from the west and was being silhouetted by the moon behind it for now. Bright shafts of light came through the cracks in the clouds like light through a window with half broken blinds.

They had no communications directly with the pilot or crew of the helicopter, so they led them to the site by relaying messages through the Duluth Airport. Tom struggled with the plane, and Laurie kept up the radio communications.

The pilot of the rescue chopper had a paramedic on board for medical attention if it was needed, but the rescue person would be lowered first to prepare a landing site if possible. The powerful searchlight scanned the ground until they picked up Julie's body and Jake. Timmy was under her now, so they couldn't see him, but Tom and Laurie had said that there were two people there.

Eetah heard the chopper coming and he rose and walked quickly away from Julie and Timmy. Airplanes usually scared him. Not enough to make him run away, but this chopper was more than his natural born fear could handle. He remembered his ride in a helicopter a while back, and as much as he was grateful for being cared for, he didn't want another ride. He ran back and stood with his mate, who was standing on a small ridge a short distance away. She was thoroughly confused

Bob Ewing was the coast guard rescuer, who would prepare the site. He was lowered, along with a crate that contained a chain saw, blankets, a radio, and other equipment he might need. There weren't a lot of trees to contend with, just a lot of brush, which was about five feet high. As soon as Bob hit the ground fifty feet from Julie, he lit a flare to mark his spot and then made his way to the site to check on the people.

Bob's flashlight beam, bobbing as he walked, showed the people in the chopper his progress over toward Julie, the light playing out on the ground in front of him. It was Jake that he saw first. He was standing and wagging his tail as if someone had just come into the yard to play with him. Bob put out his hand and Jake licked it and then jumped up on him licking his face and almost knocking him over backward. Then he turned and ran back to Julie as if he were showing Bob the way.

Bob bent over Julie and shined his light in her face. Her lips and cheeks were tinged with blue and she was comatose, but when he shined the light on her chest, he could see the slow rise and fall of her meager respirations. Timmy's head was next to hers, and he moaned as Bob shined the light in his face. "They're alive," Bob radioed to the pilot. "Get Carney down here." Carney was Carnell Williams, the paramedic on board. Both men had participated in many rescues, most of them on Lake Superior. They were ready for whatever the situation required. They had preformed rescues on the big lake under the worst of conditions so this one was almost routine.

Carney was off and running the minute he hit the ground. Bob tied Jake up to a tree to keep him out of the way. He wasn't happy about that and he barked constantly. Carney's first examination of Timmy showed hypothermia, and a dislocated shoulder, along with numerous cuts and bruises, but his vital signs were stable, so he quickly turned his attention to Julie.

Julie was only taking about three breaths per minute. Her heart rate was less that twenty beats a minute, and her body temperature was in the low eighties. An electric heating bag that would raise her body temperature had been dropped with Carney, and he quickly stripped off the rest of her wet clothing and got her into the bag. Carney had never seen anyone so badly beat up. Her body was covered with bruises, cuts, and scratches. The wound under her arm was still badly infected and open. Her breast and side were covered with scabs and open sores. She was in very bad shape and he knew it was going to be touch and go from here on in.

Timmy was also stripped and put in the same bag with Julie for the time being. He showed some signs of waking up, and maybe being next to her would help him emotionally if he did awaken. They needed to get them both on board as soon as possible.

While Carney cared for the victims, Bob clear-cut an area about fifty feet in diameter for the chopper to land. He placed flares ninety degrees apart to mark four sides of the clearing, and he scampered out of the way as the big chopper set down.

Julie and Timmy were put onto a stretcher, which resembled a big wire basket, and the two burly coast guard men carried them through the brush to the helicopter and shoved them aboard. Then Carney got an IV started in Julie and plugged in the heaters on the warming bag, while Bob returned to the site for one last look around and to retrieve Jake, who was becoming frantic. Once untied, the big dog jerked the rope from Bob's hands and raced to the chopper, leaping almost five feet into the air and through the open door, almost knocking Carney over in the process. He wasn't going to be left behind.

Bob could find no sign of anybody else and no possessions, so he returned to the chopper to leave. He was far enough away yet from the big bird, and the whoosh of the props as they idled was muffled enough, that he heard the howl of the two wolves in the woods behind him. He turned and ran the rest of the way, throwing the last of the equipment inside, and jumped in, pulling the door shut behind him. "Spooky down there, Carney, did you hear those wolves?"

Carney was on the radio to the hospital, so Bob said nothing more as he proceeded to tie Jake in the back. He gave the dog just enough rope to reach Julie's head, where he wanted to be and the chopper was up and airborne once again, heading to the hospital.

Meanwhile, Tom and Laurie were just lining up to land at the airport. Tom brought the aircraft around and set it down as light as a feather, and they taxied over to the hanger where a maintenance worker was waiting for them.

"Hey, you guys are late tonight," he quipped. "Hope you were behaving yourselves." They both let the remark pass, but Laurie gave him a disgusted look, and walked into the hanger.

They hadn't had a chance to talk much in the plane because of the noise. Now, as they sat down in the break room with coffee, Tom looked at Laurie. All of the excitement had gotten his curiosity up and he had decided, to hell with bowling.

He began with,. "That wolf with the collar, was that the one you were looking for? Was he the one that had the broken leg a year ago? I wonder why he attacked those people. I wonder where they came from."

Laurie was deep in thought but she became alert long enough to turn to Tom and say, "I'm sure the wolf was the same one we were looking for, and I don't think he attacked them. Let's get over to the hospital and see what we can find out." Both of them got out of their coveralls and into their street clothes and ran to Tom's car. Laurie made a call on her cell phone and found out that the victims were being brought into Duluth General, and that's all they knew right now. It was only about a mile away, and they were there before the chopper landed.

Julie's vital signs hadn't changed much, but she didn't seem to be getting any worse, and they were only about ten minutes away now. Timmy was conscious, but appeared to be traumatized by the whole event and just clung to Julie, not saying a word. Carney asked him his name, but Timmy only stared at him.

While attaching the monitoring leads to Julie, Carney cleaned her chest with alcohol wipes and noticed that she was covered with long white coarse hair that seemed to come from some animal. He looked over at Jake and ran his hands through the big dog's mane, looking at the fine yellow fur that came off in his hands. This fur wasn't from the dog. She had no shirt on when they got there, just a pair of tattered jeans and a bra. Was it possible she had a fur coat somewhere?

The news of the rescue had preceded the landing of the chopper, and the media was already at the hospital. It wasn't known yet who these people were, but the only people missing and unaccounted for were Arnie Bottelmiller, his companion Julie Feldman, and his son Timmy. Oh, and their dog. They had been missing for going on two weeks now, on a flight to Thunder Bay, Canada.

Arnie was completely out of it now. He hadn't been conscious for almost a day. He was severely dehydrated and suffering from a raging infection which had spread from his buttocks into his bloodstream, poisoning his entire body. In his lap lay the pad and pen he had been writing with before he passed out. The pad was turned to the last page, and the writing was shaky and hard to read:

My dearest Julie,

Before I go, I want you to know that nothing in this world mattered to me as much as you and Timmy. You were my reason for living, and I can only hope and pray that you both made it out safely. I don't know everything that is wrong with me right now, but I know my time has come, and I am very sick. I want you to know, sweetheart, that I am not in pain, just very aware of what is happening. I have made my peace with God, and I hope he will welcome me into His Heaven, where I will save a spot for you and Timmy. I love you so much and am so sorry for what happened.

Arnie

It was nearly dark when he last woke up and wrote it. The writing was smeary, hard to read, and he tore the paper in one place. Arnie had given up, and all of the animosity he experienced in the last few days was gone. He was at peace with himself.

As soon as the helicopter was on the pad, hospital personnel grabbed Julie and Timmy and whisked them down to the emergency room. Timmy was sedated until they could fully examine him, and sent up to a private room to sleep. For what he had been through, his vital signs were good and his body temperature was around ninety-six degrees. Carnie had reduced his shoulder back in place on the way back.

Julie's body temperature was slowly rising, and was now in the low nineties. The only question was whether she had suffered any brain damage from the low flow of blood. Her body had been so cold that her heart was barely pumping when she was found. She was still in ICU, and a nurse was stationed at her bedside in case she woke up.

At first Julie thought she must have died, and the bright lights were the ones that everyone saw as they climbed that shaft of light to the world beyond, but she could hear voices, and the lights were not in beams, but just above her. Her eyes started fluttering and she was aware of someone leaning over her and talking, but she couldn't understand them. Julie said one word and she said it only once but very clearly: "Arnie." Then it got all foggy again.

The nurse rang for help and the emergency room doctor in charge came in. "She was with me for a second, Doctor," she said. "She said the name Arnie."

The phone rang at Irv's house in Blue Lake at a quarter past midnight. "This is the Duluth Police Department calling from Duluth General Hospital. Sir, we have been given your name by the police as the contact person for the people missing from your area in a plane that disappeared."

"Yes, yes!" Irv nearly shouted. "Did you find them? Are they all right?"

"Sir, all I can tell you is we have recovered a young lady and a small boy from the wilderness area about eighty miles northwest of here. She's in critical condition right now with hypothermia and injuries. The boy is physically fine, but mentally unresponsive. Could you come to the hospital right away to help with identification?"

"Yes, I can. I will fly in and be there in about an hour."

"We will have a squad car meet you at the airport. And would you bring a dog carrier for a big yellow dog we think is theirs?"

"Yes!" Irv shouted as he pulled on his coveralls and was out the door. He stopped for a moment. *Arnie, they had said nothing about Arnie.* He took off running again. *Where was Arnie?* He dialed the cell phone as he was running down the road. He was calling Shirley Capes.

Tom and Laurie identified themselves at the hospital and asked about the victims.

"The woman is in critical condition, suffering from hypothermia," they were told by the doctor. "The boy seems to be fine, physically."

"Was there any evidence they were attacked by animals?" Laurie asked.

"I don't think so," the doctor answered. "She had a lot of scrapes and cuts and a deep wound under her arm and a rather bad scrape on her breast, but animal bites or claw marks? I don't think so. Why do you ask?"

"There was an animal in the area when we spotted them."

"What kind of animal?" the doctor asked.

Laurie looked at the floor and did not answer at first. Finally, she looked up and said. "A wolf."

CHAPTER 15

▼

Irv had so many questions he had forgotten to ask, the most critical being, where was Arnie? There wasn't any answer at Shirley's house, but someone had picked up the phone and then dropped it disconnecting them. He didn't try again.

Irv rented a place right across the road from the airfield when he stayed at the airport. He was out the door, running across the road and down the airport driveway before he was done dressing. The runway lights were on, but there was nobody stationed at the airport during the night. He went in the side door of the hanger he rented and flicked the lights on, pushing the door opener at the same time. His yellow and blue Piper Cub was always ready to go, so he jumped in and fired up the engine. He let it warm for a second while he checked all of his equipment and stowed the old dog carrier he had dug out of the back of the hanger. Then he taxied out onto the runway, hitting the door closer behind him. He checked in with the control tower, which recorded all messages after ten o'clock at night, leaving a message that he was heading for Duluth.

When Irv first left the house, there were a few snowflakes coming down, but now, as he sped down the runway and lifted skyward, it was starting to come down pretty heavily. He would try to gain some altitude as soon as he could and get above the snow to keep it off his wings and keep the plane from icing up. It seemed to have gone from fall to winter in just the last couple of days, and this looked like the first icy blast of the season. The radio gave some subdued background static, but otherwise only the drone of the engine interrupted his thoughts. Below him the lights of Blue Lake flickered and disappeared.

He thought back to all the fishing and hunting trips he and Arnie had taken over the years and remembered all of the good times they had together. He remained cordial with Julie, but he resented the time that she stole away from that friendship. Now it was time to put those thoughts away and do what he could to bring them home. It was then that his cell phone rang.

"This is Irv," he shouted above the engine noise.

"This is Shirley," the slurred voice said back. "Did you call? I was sleeping and ..."

"Yes! Yes!" Irv shouted. "I'm on my way to Duluth. They found Julie and Timmy and the dog, but so far no word on Arnie. I don't have a number or I would call them back, but I should be there in less than an hour. Can you meet me at the airport? The police will take us to them."

"I'll be there," Shirley said. She got unsteadily to her feet and walked along the wall to the bathroom. *It was a bad time to be drunk,* 'she thought' *but what the hell, she could still drive. She had done some of her best driving when she was drunk.*

It had snowed about six inches since nightfall and it was starting to accumulate. Arnie's plane was no longer visible from the air. It looked like it was part of the tree it was sitting under. The temperature had fallen below freezing, but the cool temperatures had helped him to hang on a while longer, because his biggest enemy right now was his raging fever. The cold air had helped lower his body temperature. He still remained unresponsive and was oblivious to what was happening around him.

Julie's mental function was off and on all night. Several times it looked like she was on the verge of waking up, and then she would slip back into oblivion again. Her body temperature was back to normal and she was being given massive amounts of antibiotics for the infection that raged under her arm. The plan was for them to operate as soon as she was stable. They would open up the wound and clean it out, as x rays showed foreign matter still in there.

At three-fifteen a.m. Irv touched down and taxied over to the main terminal where airport handlers pulled his plane away. He ran into the building where he was met by a uniformed police officer from the Duluth Police Department, who told him a car was waiting. He was also met by Shirley Capes, who was sitting at a table drinking black coffee. She had made it without incident but the police were less than happy with her. Quickly they were on their way to the hospital a mile away through the icy streets in the patrol car. When they arrived at the hospital Shirley stayed in the lobby with the police, while Irv went upstairs.

Irv was not sure at first if he was looking at Julie or not. This woman looked like she'd been thrown off a mountain. Her face was covered with an oxygen mask, and it seemed like everything else was bandaged. He sat down beside the bed and took her hand. It was covered with cuts and bruises and still felt cold to the touch. He brushed back her hair, and softly said her name.

Julie was right on the edge, and she heard a voice call her name. "Arnie, it that you?" she mumbled.

"Julie, it's Irv," he answered. "Where is Arnie?"

It was as if a bell had gone off in her head, and Julie opened her eyes wide looking straight at Irv. "He's on the island," she said, and then she slipped back to sleep.

Irv was out of the room and across the hall to the nurse's station, asking for a phone to use. He had left his cell phone on the plane. He was calling the coast guard station and asking to speak to the men who were on the rescue team that brought Julie and Timmy in. "There's still one more in the woods," he said. "Julie told me that he's still out there, if I could only talk to the people who picked her up."

"The pilot and the rescuer have gone home, but the paramedic who treated her is still here. Would you like to talk to him?"

"Yes, please," Irv said.

"Carney Williams," the voice on the phone said, as Irv drummed his fingers nervously on the desktop in the nurse's station.

"Carney, my name is Irv Engstrom. I'm from Blue Lake, Minnesota, and I'm a friend of the people you guys rescued late last night. Carney, those people were the survivors of a plane crash. Or at least I think it crashed. There is still one more person out there. There were three people and a dog in that plane. You guys know where she, the boy, and the dog were at, and I think Arnie, that's the other one, might be close by. It's been nearly two weeks now and the weather is getting bad."

"Irv, where can I reach you?" Carney interrupted him.

Irv gave him the number of the phone without even asking if it was o.k. It had to be alright, that's all there was to it.

The phone rang a few minutes later, and the nursing supervisor handed it to Irv with a stern look that said. *This shit has to stop.*

"Irv, this is Carney Williams getting back to you. I just checked with my supervisor and told him what you said, and he is calling the other two people back in. How quickly can you get over here to go with us?"

Irv asked directions to the coast guard base, from the police officer who had just come upstairs with Shirley. He showed him the address he had written and said, "How long?"

The officer said, "A half-hour."

"I heard him," Carney said. "We'll be waiting for you."

Shirley would stay at the hospital with Julie, although she had never really known her, while Irv and the police officer ran down the stairs and jumped back into the squad.

It was Irv's first experience riding on a red-light run in a squad car, on streets as slick as snot, and his knuckles were white gripping the dashboard. The only words Irv said all the way over were, "Holy shit" and "Oh, my God," as the car skidded up the main gate. The guards at the gate waved them through, and Carney Williams met him and they ran to the still warming-up chopper.

"Let's get aboard and we can talk on the way," he said shouting over the noise of the prop.

"I want to get out of here before they ground us," the pilot said looking over his shoulder to Irv. "Dave Cousins," he said, extending his hand. "This weather is marginal, but let's see if we can spot anything."

"Irv Engstrom," Irv said shaking hands. "Dave, all we know is the woman you picked up last night was awake just long enough to tell us that Arnie's on an island. I have to believe that there are not that many islands to check out, and if we start where you found her and work in a circle out from there, we could find him."

Only Bob had got there in time to accompany Carney, Irv and the pilot, and they all looked at the map as they flew back over the wilderness area. Irv believed that Julie was trying to get out, to go for help, and when he looked at the black X that Dave put on the map, he almost had to think they came from the north. Going south was the only way out. There were no islands in Borden Lake, with the exception of some big rocks, and it was close to the lake where Julie and Timmy had been found. He flew up the Sawbuck River, as there were two lakes just north of there, Rainbow and Kato. Rainbow was dotted with islands, but there were only two islands in Kato.

Eetah and his mate saw the big chopper go over again. Things had settled down after all the excitement last night, and this time they wanted no part of it and they headed for the swamps to hide. His mate was coming into season and their friendship was now more of a courtship. They were becoming very close. He was busy marking out an area for their family, hopefully a good-sized litter.

The islands on Rainbow Lake were many, but they were also small, and within a half-hour, they had checked them all as well as they could with the searchlights.

They were going to go up to Kato when the radio gave a tone and Dave answered it. Irv could see the concern on his face as he listened in his earphones, but Irv couldn't hear the other side of the conversation.

"We have to leave," Dave said. "The storm is getting worse and they are calling us in."

"Let's catch Kato and then go," Irv said. "Please, Dave." Irv was begging them

"Well, I don't know. It's kind of out of the way. Oh, hell," he said and swung the big ship around. Carney grinned and didn't say a word. Bob just looked out the window.

They were over Kato in a few minutes and speeding down to the other end of the lake where the islands were. The visibility dropped to about one hundred feet, so Dave had to bring the chopper in as low as he could and still stay out of the trees. They circled the island twice and saw nothing at first. Then they heard Bob's breathe catch. "Dave, there's what looks to be an airplane float on the beach down there."

Dave brought the big chopper down within a few feet of the water and, sure enough, it was a float off a plane. It was off of Arnie's plane, just where Julie had left it. He slowly brought the big chopper around as their back was to the island and they were looking down at Arnie's plane.

There wasn't any place to set down, and it was too risky to hover where they were with the wind blowing them around, so Dave took the chopper back up while they formulated a plan. They decided to drop Bob down with the winch. He could radio back up if Arnie was there and then they would talk about what to do next.

The radio sounded again and Dave told the base they were on their way, but his look told Irv not to worry. It took a few minutes for Bob to get everything ready, and they were soon hovering back over the island. Dave lowered the chopper until Bob signaled him to stop. He slid out the door while Carney played out the winch. It was getting colder by the minute and the inside of the aircraft was getting soaked with snow blowing in the open door. The winch stopped and Carney started bringing it back up before it got snagged on something down there. Dave held the chopper steady, but there was a look of concern on his face that said. *This better work or we're going to be in deep shit.*

When Bob hit the ground, he was right on the beach, so he unhooked the cable and made his way through the underbrush to the plane. There was wreckage from the plane scattered everywhere, but the first thing he noticed was the broken-off wing shoved up to the passenger door and wedged in the opening. It had stayed in place even after the plane had slid down the tree. The windows were covered with snow so he couldn't see inside.

Standing on the ground, Bob was looking at the lower half of the door.. The ground was littered with garbage and beer bottles, and he had to kick some of it aside to keep from slipping on something. Reaching as high as he could, he grabbed the handle and pulled on the door. A small avalanche of snow fell on him as the door jerked open on its bent hinges.

Arnie was leaning toward the door, and Bob had to react quickly to keep him from spilling out of the plane on top of him. He put his hand on Arnie's shoulder to keep him in place. Arnie's head was down with his chin resting on his chest, and Bob couldn't tell if he was breathing or not. The smell from the aircraft and the man's rotting flesh told him he was possibly dealing with a cadaver, but he didn't look dead. Bob grabbed the handheld radio and said," Dave, get Carney down here right now."

CHAPTER 16

▼

They opened the door on the passenger side so Carney could get in with Arnie, and his initial examination showed that he was indeed alive, but barely. He was having trouble breathing and his blood pressure was very low, so low that Carney could hardly get a reading on the lower end of the scale. The stench made Carney gag and he fought the reflexes that wanted to get rid of everything he had eaten for the last two days.

The mystery was why Arnie was still in the plane and why he didn't escape with Julie and his son. Carney checked out Arnie's lower extremities and as much of his body as he could under the circumstances, and then he slid his hands around Arnie and felt the broken spinal cord bulging from his back. *That's why he was still here*, he said to himself. *His back is broken.*

In the chopper, Dave was struggling to keep the craft in the area. Winds were gusting to fifty miles an hour, buffeting the big helicopter and threatening to drive it into the lake. Irv knelt in the doorway trying to see what was going on below, but the visibility was almost zero. Dave warned him not to get too close to the opening, even though he had safety a harness on. If he fell there was no one left to pull him back in

The radio sounded again, and the base was warning them to leave the area immediately, if they hadn't already done so. The problem was only going to be worse on the way back, as the wind and snow coming off Lake Superior created an almost horizontal snowstorm. Dave could stall no longer. He radioed back that they had found the wreckage and believed they might have a survivor. They would leave as soon as they finished checking it out.

Carney called back up to Dave and told him to drop a backboard and the wire stretcher, because their victim was going to have to be immobilized before he could be moved. They had to hurry. His condition was very fragile. Irv helped tie the stretcher and board to the cable, and then he lowered it down, hoping he was somewhere near the people below.

After a few minutes when Carney hadn't seen the basket yet, he radioed Dave again to send it down. Dave said the cable was slack. It was on the ground somewhere and they had better find it fast before it got snagged in the trees. Just then the big ship lurched from a wind gust, and the stretcher and board bounced from the water where they had fallen, and landed almost at Bob's feet.

Carney was able to get the board secure on Arnie by sliding the board behind him, and the back of the seat. As soon as all the straps were tight and Arnie's head was secure in the protective collar, Carney turned Arnie ninety degrees in the seat so his back was to the open door, and gently lowered him into Bob's open arms. Bob held Arnie's upper body stable until Carney could get out of the plane and come around to help him. They lowered him to the ground and into the Stokes basket, wrapping him in blankets. Almost immediately he was covered with snow.

They carried Arnie to the shoreline where they had to look once more for the cable. The aircraft had moved away from the island and farther over the lake to keep the cable out of the trees, and slowly Carney talked Dave backward toward them. The bright searchlight illuminated the cable and Bob waded out into the frigid lake and grabbed it before it got lost again. They snapped on the line, and Carney gave them the order to bring it up. Bob rode on top of the basket, as he would have to help them line up with the aircraft door as soon as they got high enough. The basket was swinging in the wind, and Bob had to hold on with all his might to keep from being pitched into the lake fifty feet below.

Earlier Irv had put on the harness, with Dave's instructions, that kept him tethered to the chopper. He was now standing in the doorway holding a long fireman's pole with a hook on the end waiting for the stretcher. It seemed to take forever, but at last it came into view, and Irv reached out with the pole and hooked the cable, letting it slide through the hook until the stretcher was level with the door. He then hooked the end of the stretcher and pulled it into the doorway close enough for Bob to jump aboard, and then helped him slide it the rest of the way and latch it to the deck.

As soon as the stretcher was latched down, the cable was dropped once more for Carney. Arnie was wrapped in blankets, including his head, and Bob left him wrapped up until they wrestled Carney through the doorway. He was soaking wet and covered with slush.

Irv had never seen such an unselfish, heroic act as these people performed this morning, and his eyes were brimming with tears as Bob slammed the door shut. Dave signaled to give the ship full throttle and shouted "Let's get the hell out of here."

Irv knelt on the floor as Carney uncovered the upper half of Arnie's body. His eyes were closed and his breathing was more of a snort than anything. Carney washed his face and strapped an oxygen mask on him. He asked Irv to hold Arnie's arm while he started an I.V. to get some fluids into his body. It was about all they could do for now. Once the I.V. was started, Irv laid Arnie's arm down, but he still continued to sit and hold his hand and pray.

The big chopper was being tossed around like a toy in the storm, and sometimes it felt as if they were standing still, in a pushing match against the storm. Then the wind would die down for a second, and the craft would lurch forward as if it regained some newfound traction. Dave tried to get enough altitude to get above the worst of the weather, but wasn't able to, so he came back down to three thousand feet and leveled off. The airport called and told them they had them on radar and gave Dave some new headings, because they were badly off course.

Carney sat with his back to the wall and watched his patient, and Irv remained next to Arnie, still holding his hand. Carney unzipped his jacket and took out a pad of paper that he had grabbed before leaving the wrecked airplane. "Irv, I found this in his lap and thought you could give it to him when he's better."

Irv looked at the pad and said, "Thanks." He slid it into his jacket.

They weren't going to be able to land at the hospital in this storm, so an ambulance was dispatched to the air base to stand by until they landed.

It took two hours from the time they left the crash site to arrive at the airport, and the sun was just rising in the east. It was a good thing they were in a helicopter, because the runways were blocked with snowdrifts, and all air traffic had been canceled shortly after they had taken off.

They loaded Arnie into the back of the ambulance, and Irv jumped in with them while Carney brought the doctor that was aboard up to speed on what he knew about Arnie's condition. Then Carney gave Irv's shoulder a squeeze, jumped out, and closed the door. Following behind a giant snowplow from the city, they headed for the hospital.

As soon as Arnie was taken into the emergency ward, Irv went upstairs to check on Julie. When he peeked around the door to her room, he saw Timmy sitting on the end of her bed. Julie was sitting up, looking like she had been ridden hard and put away wet, but at least she was conscious and smiling weakly. The news about Arnie hadn't preceded him, and Irv took her hand and told her that they had found him, and that he was in the emergency ward downstairs right now, and that they were doing everything possible for him.

"How did you find him?" Julie asked.

"You told us, sweetheart," Irv said.

"I did? How did they find Timmy and me?"

"I don't know the whole story yet," Irv said, "but I sure intend to find out."

While they were talking, there was a knock on the door and a petite brunette in a Department of Natural Resources uniform stuck her head around the corner, asking if she could come in.

"My name is Laurie," she said. "I couldn't rest until I met you and saw how you were."

"Please come in," Julie said. "Did you rescue us?"

Laurie approached the bed. "No.—No, I wish I could take the credit for that but I can't. My partner and I spotted you and the boy." She paused a second and ran her hand through Timmy's hair. "We would have never found you, but we were tracking wolves through their radio collars, and one of them happened to be really close to you." How close Laurie did not say.

"Where's my dog?" Julie asked.

"He came back with you guys in the chopper," Irv said. "I'll find out for you, but I know he's here because the hospital called and asked if I could bring a carrier and take him home with me."

"That dog saved our lives," Julie said. "When Timmy went into the river, Jake pulled him to shore, and before that when we were so hungry and we couldn't go any further, Jake killed a deer and shared it with us."

"Jake killed a deer?" Laurie asked.

"Yes, a fawn," she said.

In Laurie's mind it was all falling into place. She knew what she had seen with the wolf. He had been providing cover for Julie when they found them, and she knew who killed the deer. She would never be able to prove it and wasn't going to try, but she was pretty sure she knew what happened.

Arnie's mother was notified and was on her way to the hospital right now, in Julie's Jeep, driven by a neighbor that Irv had called. She had sat in that rocking chair looking out the window for as long as her son had sat in that plane seat waiting to be rescued. She never lost faith. Julie's parents had also been notified by Julie herself, but wouldn't be able to come down until the weather broke.

Before evening Julie asked to get up and was taken down to the intensive care ward to see Arnie. He had just gotten out of surgery, where they removed the dead flesh from his bottom, and installed a brace on his back that would hold things in place until they could do surgery to fuse his spine. He was going to be paralyzed from the waist down, possibly for the rest of his life, but his vital signs were improving and it looked like he was going to beat the infection. He wouldn't be awake for a while, but Julie asked if she could comb his hair and just sit with him.

She was still weak with her own injuries and was going to have surgery of her own in the morning to clean up the wound under her arm, so she was escorted back to her room after a short time. When she got to her room, Irv was sitting in a chair by the window with Jake at his feet. It took some talking, but Irv convinced the nurses and doctors how important it was for Julie to see Jake, so they gave the dog a one-time pass. Julie sat on the bed and the big dog jumped up and licked her face until it was sopping wet. Was it Jake's saliva or Julie's tears? It was a little of both.

EPILOGUE

▼

Timmy was well enough to go home with his grandmother the next morning along with Jake, but Julie would have to stay a few more days. The storm blew itself out by noon and the next day the roads were open, the sun was shining and it all started to melt away. Arnie would be in the hospital for at least two weeks while they did some skin grafts on his bottom and stabilized his back. After that there would be a lot of therapy.

The injury in Julie's armpit had been cleaned out and sewn up. She lost a couple of glands, but otherwise was no worse for wear. She had also lost twenty-one pounds, and for someone who was in near-perfect shape before the accident, that was a lot. She looked very gaunt.

Shirley had stayed at the hospital all night in a rented room and the next morning she went to look in on Arnie. They were using a guest columnist for a few weeks, but she assured him that they were waiting anxiously for his first column. She was going to be gone for a while herself, as she was making arrangements to get some help with a couple of personal problems.

Arnie gave her a weak smile and said, "Shirley, look in the top drawer of that nightstand." Irv had left Arnie his pad of paper from the plane before he left the hospital that morning, with Timmy and Arnie's mother, on their way home.

"Shirley paged through the writings and said, "My God, Arnie, there's two weeks work here." With that, she did something she had never done before: she leaned over and kissed him.

"Sure, now that my boys are paralyzed you try to put the moves on me," Arnie laughed.

"You know what, Arnie? Maybe part of you is dead right now, but the part we all love is still here, and I for one am so very grateful." Shirley tapped him on the head with the pad of paper he had given her.

"Hey before you take that, give me the last page," Arnie said. He crumpled the paper and dropped it into the wastebasket. His note to Julie would not be needed now. He would rather tell her to her face, and he fully intended to do just that as soon as they could get a minister to do the ceremony.

Irv was eventually hired by the newspaper to be the company pilot. Most people said he spent most of his time just flying Arnie around the countryside. Insurance had paid to replace the plane and Shirley Capes paid to have a wheelchair ramp built on Arnie's dock and a special seat built in the new plane for him so he could sit right next to Irv. It wasn't the same as flying it himself, but he was still in the air and was able to continue on with his writing. He also had his own parking space at the newspaper right next to the editor.

Although she knew better than to ask Arnie not to fly again, Julie vowed she would never fly again. But she didn't really have time now, anyway because she was busy with Timmy, and through the miracle of science, had a new baby on the way to get ready for.

As for Timmy, his world would always be a special place that few others would understand. That is other than Julie and Arnie. Each and everyday they spent with Timmy they thanked God for their wonderful, special child. They would never forget what he went through in the forest. He was their little hero.

Shirley Capes turned over the reigns as the paper editor to her assistant. She did a lot of traveling now and looked very good for her age. Quitting smoking and drinking had helped her figure a lot, and hardly a week went by that her and Arnie didn't get together for coffee and rolls at Grandmas café. Arnie would always smile at the waitress and say, "Give me the check. She's retired."

As for Jake, Arnie could never get the big dog back in his airplane again so he just quit trying. *Julie must have had a talk with him*, he thought.

'And' one hundred miles northwest of them on a cold winter's night, a love affair had been consummated. Seven wolf cubs would be formed from this union, and it would be Eetah's first family. They would also be the start of a new wolf pack that Eetah and his mate would rule over for a very long time.

The end.

978-0-595-44945-:
0-595-44945-X